SEVEN SLEEPERS **THE LOST CHRONICLES** 2

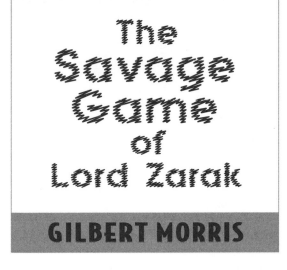

The Savage Game of Lord Zarak

GILBERT MORRIS

MOODY PRESS
CHICAGO

© 2000 by
GILBERT MORRIS

Library of Congress Cataloging-in-Publication Data

Morris, Gilbert
    The savage game of Lord Zarak / by Gilbert Morris.
        p. cm. -- (the lost chronicles ; v #2)
    Summary: The Seven Sleepers must confront an evil king whose sport
is to offer the prisoners in his dungeon one chance at freedom by
escaping past his savage hunting dogs.
    ISBN 0-8024-3668-4 (pbk.)
    [1. Fantasy. 2. Christian life--Fiction.] I. Title

PZ7.M8279 Sav 2000
[Fic]--dc21
                                                            99-058292

            1 3 5 7 9 10 8 6 4 2

Printed in the United States of America

Contents

1
The Stranger

Sarah Collingwood took a deep breath, filled her lungs with air, and bent her body. Then she dove into the blue-green waters of the bay and kicked with her fins. The water was as warm as a bath. In front of her she could see Josh Adams swimming downward toward the reef.

Maybe sometimes Josh is awkward on land, Sarah thought, *but he's sure a great swimmer!*

The two were down ten or twelve feet now. They passed a huge school of brilliantly colored fish—red, green, yellow, orange, and more—more colors, it seemed, than in a rainbow. Then they swam by an enormous fish that Josh had told Sarah was a sea bass. He looked big enough to take off one's leg, but he hung suspended in the beautiful green water, simply fanning his fins and tail gently.

Sarah loved to scuba dive. Back in Oldworld, her parents had once taken her to the coast of Belize, where the second largest barrier reef in the world was located. As usual, when she thought of the way life was before the world had been practically destroyed by atomic warfare, it made her sad. But then she glanced at Josh, who had suddenly stopped to investigate something, and she thought, *But now I'm one of the Seven Sleepers, and I've got six good friends, and I've got Goél. I just won't think about the past.*

Goél. Since being awakened from the sleep capsules that had saved them from the atomic war, the Seven Sleepers had served Goél. He was a mysterious but noble figure. He led an ongoing battle against the Dark Lord, who had set out to enslave Nuworld.

Josh was still looking at something. He turned toward her and gestured wildly.

She looked to where he pointed—toward the reef —and could see a shadowy shape. Shock ran along her nerves. She did not know what the shape was, but Josh was obviously alarmed. She followed him as he swiftly swam upward, his fins thrashing. When they broke the surface, he yelled, "That's a barracuda down there! He could take a plug out of you."

Sarah was not as afraid of barracudas as Josh seemed to be. She had never heard of a barracuda attacking a human being, although they did look vicious. "Come on, Josh! Let's go back down and pull his tail!" she joked.

"Are you crazy?" Josh had shoved his mask back from his face and now wiped the water away. "Those things look like they're bad tempered."

"Well, come on. I'll race you to shore, then."

They swam toward the beach, and it was easy with the flippers on. Sarah did not even have to use her arms but, with legs thrashing, just drove herself forward. Since she was keeping her head high, she could see that the other Sleepers were playing volleyball on the beach. When she got close in, she pulled off her flippers and waded the rest of the way. She was careful not to step on any jellyfish, for she was very sensitive to them.

"Hey, you didn't wait for us!" Josh called to the volleyball players. He tossed his flippers and mask onto the blanket where he had been lying earlier, getting a tan. "How do you expect to win without your star player?"

There were three players on one side: Dave Cooper, the oldest of the Sleepers, at the age of fifteen; Jake Garfield, thirteen, with short red hair; and Abigail Roberts, a blue-eyed blonde who was, in the opinion of some, the prettiest girl around.

On the other side of the net stood Bob Lee Jackson and Wash Jones. Bob Lee was never called anything but "Reb." Although he wore only swimming trunks, he had his cowboy hat perched on top of his tow-colored hair. His light blue eyes squinted in the sun as he said, "Why don't you all go on back and swim? We don't need help. We're beating these folks like a drum."

Wash Jones was standing close to the net. He was the youngest of the Sleepers and the most cheerful. His white teeth now gleamed in his dark face as he said, "Aw, you can come and help us, Sarah. We need somebody good-looking over here to balance out us ugly folks."

With a laugh Sarah went to Reb and Wash's side of the net. "All right," she said.

But Josh said, "Aw, I think I'll just go lie down and watch you guys play." He walked toward his blanket.

Sarah's close friend Josh Adams was very tall for almost fifteen. She knew that he was also very shy and unsure of himself, although he tried to keep this covered up for the most part.

"Come on," Reb yelled. "Let's see what you all can do."

The volleyball game went on for some time. There was a lot of laughter, and no one really cared much who won.

Finally, from the sidelines Josh called, "I vote we cook us some hamburgers."

"Yeah!" Reb said. "That sounds good to me. You girls get to cooking!"

Abbey made a face at him. "Who died and made you king?" she said. "You can cook as well as I can!"

In the final event, the boys built the fire and set up the homemade grill. The girls made the hamburgers. Soon the burgers were sizzling, and when they were cooked, all the Sleepers sat down on the sand.

Reb Jackson put his between two slices of bread and scowled in disapproval. "Sure wish we had some real hamburger buns," he complained. "Don't seem like a hamburger with just putting it on bread."

"Tastes all right to me," Jake said. He took a huge bite, chewed, and then winked at Wash. "If Reb ever gets married, his wife will have an awful time. He demands the best of everything."

"I'd hate to be married to *him*," Abbey said. She was taking dainty little bites and chewing them thoroughly. The sun caught at her blonde hair, making it seem there were threads of gold in it. "He's impossible!"

"No. I'm possible," Reb said. "I'm so possible I can't tell you how possible I am. As a matter of fact, I'm the most normal person I know. Everybody else is abnormal."

Dave laughed aloud. "If you're normal, and we're all abnormal, then we'll have to put you in a cage. Because when all the abnormal people outnumber the normal people, then they become normal."

This foolishness went on until suddenly Josh glanced back toward the woods behind them and said, "Who is that? I never saw him before."

Sarah looked. Someone was walking toward them from the trees.

"Neither did I," Abbey said. Then her eyes narrowed, and she murmured to Sarah, "But whoever he is, he sure is good-looking, isn't he?"

Sarah was not surprised that Abbey would at once analyze the newcomer as far as looks were concerned. She was slightly boy crazy and had been so ever since they had come to Nuworld. Many of their troubles had been the result of Abbey's fondness for good-looking boys.

Josh got up and walked toward the stranger. "Hello," he said. "You looking for someone?"

"I'm looking for the Seven Sleepers, and I guess you're it."

The speaker was more than six feet tall. He was young—eighteen or so. He had reddish hair and wide-spaced green eyes. He was tanned, he was indeed handsome, and he appeared to be very strong. He was wearing a pair of light tan slacks, a white shirt, and a pair of low-cut, tan half boots. "My name's Roland Winters."

"I'm Josh Adams, and this is Sarah Collingwood. This is Abbey Roberts and Dave Cooper and Jake Garfield. This tall guy here is Reb Jackson, and this is Wash Jones."

Roland Winters let his eyes run over the group as if he wasn't too pleased with what he saw. "I didn't expect you to be so young," he said.

Somehow his remark irritated Sarah, but Josh just said, "People often say that. Sorry to disappoint you. But what can we do for you?"

"Nothing." Roland Winters grinned. "It's what I can do for you."

Sarah glanced back at Josh and saw the puzzled look on his face. "What does that mean?" she asked Roland Winters. "What could you do for us?"

"Well, Goél sent me."

At the name of Goél, everyone became more alert. "Goél sent you?" Jake exclaimed. "For what?"

"I guess he thought you needed some help for some reason or other, so he asked me to come and meet him here. He told me a little bit about you kids." The newcomer hesitated, then shook his head. "I've heard some stories about you, but I guess they were exaggerated. Kids like you couldn't have done as much as I hear."

The manner of Roland Winters as well as his words irritated Sarah greatly—and probably all the other Sleepers too. Good-looking and strong and able as he seemed to be, there was an arrogance about him that grated on her nerves.

"Well, if Goél sent you, I'm glad you're here," Josh said. "Join us and have a hamburger."

"Don't mind if I do." Coolly Roland Winters picked up some bread. He put some mustard and pickle on it, and made a sandwich with the meat patty. When he took a bite, he said, "Next time maybe I'll do the cooking for you. I can do a little bit better than this."

"Oh, that's just great," Reb said with a frown. "You can do all the work you want to around here. I won't stand in your way."

Roland ate two hamburgers and then some cookies that Sarah had made the day before. Apparently he found the cookies not too much to his liking, either.

Sarah grumbled to Josh, "He is so unbearable!"

"Unbearable he sure is! I just hope he's not going with us on whatever mission Goél sends us on next."

Sarah scowled. "I've got a feeling that he will be."

"What makes you think that?"

"Womanly intuition. I just feel it."

10

"And I sure hope your womanly intuition isn't right this time. In any case, he seems to be rubbing everybody the wrong way."

After they had finished eating the hamburgers and cookies, they started the volleyball game again. Nobody was really eager to have Roland Winters on their team. So he just joined in.

He wound up standing next to Sarah.

"You just set 'em up," Roland said, "and I'll knock that ball right down their throats, Sarah baby!"

"I'm not a baby!"

"Aw, come on. You almost are. How old are you anyway? Twelve?"

Sarah was so furious that she could scarcely see. She refused to answer, and the game went on.

It soon became clear to her that the annoying Roland Winters had great athletic ability. He could leap higher in the air than any of them. And when he struck the ball, the sound exploded like an artillery shell. He laughed every time he drove the ball past the opponents, which he did often.

Even so, perhaps all would have been well, but then Wash lobbed the volleyball just over the net. Roland leaped high in the air and returned it with all of his strength. The ball was nothing but a blur. It struck Wash on the forehead and knocked him down. He lay flat in the sand for a minute, unable to get up.

Sarah guessed what was going to happen next. Reb Jackson had a rather quick temper, and he had become best friends with Wash. She could see the anger flare up in Reb's face.

He ducked under the net and walked straight to Roland Winters. Without hesitation, he put a hand on the stranger's chest and gave him a shove backward.

"You didn't have to do that!" he said, his eyes blazing. "It's just a game!"

Roland did not hesitate, either. He moved so quickly that Reb had no chance to stop the blow. It caught him high on the cheekbone and knocked him down.

As Reb struggled to his feet, Dave, the largest of the Seven Sleepers—almost as tall as Roland but not nearly so heavy—came over. His face was flushed. "We don't need any bullies around here, Winters! If you're going to pick on somebody, pick on me!"

Roland did not say a word but struck out again. His fist caught Dave in the mouth, and, although Dave did not fall, he staggered backward in the sand.

Now Sarah came running. She had no chance, of course, but she beat on Roland's chest, shouting, "You leave them alone! Who do you think you are, anyway?"

Quickly the stranger pinioned her wrist and held her easily. "They started it!" he said. "If they're going to start something, they've got to take the consequences."

Next, Josh came up. "Turn her loose, Roland!" His face was pale. He glanced over to where Wash was helping Reb to his feet. He glanced at Dave and saw that his friend's mouth was bleeding. "We don't need any of this."

"You're just a bunch of babies. All of you. You can't take it."

Roland Winters turned around and stalked off down the beach. He seemed totally unconcerned about what he had done.

"What a bully!" Sarah exclaimed.

"He's hateful!" Abbey cried. She went over to Dave and said, "Let me see." Frowning, she studied his face. "Your mouth is cut. We'll have to put something on it."

As Abbey led Dave off, Sarah went to Reb. "Are you all right, Reb?"

"I reckon I'll live." But Reb's pale eyes glittered, and he added, "It's not the last of it, though."

"Aw, come on, Reb," Wash, the peacemaker, said. "We're not really hurt."

Reb did not answer. His eyes were on the form of Roland Winters, still walking away from them. "I never doubted that Goél knows what he's doing, but if he's really chosen *that* one to go with us, I reckon he's made a pretty big mistake this time."

2
Roland's Choice

For the next two days the Sleepers waited impatiently for Goél to arrive. But he did not come, and there was no guessing as to when he would appear.

In the meantime, Roland Winters proved to be the most unpleasant and arrogant bully that any of the Sleepers had ever seen. Even Wash, the most even tempered and sweet-natured of all the Sleepers, grew weary of him. And it took a great deal of tact to keep Reb Jackson from jumping into another fight, for Reb had not forgotten the blow that he had taken.

One afternoon Reb and Wash were fishing off a wharf, catching silvery, torpedo-shaped fish for supper. The setting sun seemed to be sinking right into the lake. It was a huge orange disk, and Wash said he almost expected to see the water sizzle as it went down.

"Come on, Reb, you can't go around down in the mouth for the rest of your life," he said after a while. He nudged his friend with his elbow. "We'll just hope Goél has got something else for Mr. Roland Winters to do than travel with us."

"Well, *I* sure hope so," Reb muttered. "That is one no account bird if I ever saw one. He's always bullying somebody, and he'd better not try it on me again."

"Cool off! Cool off! Can't last forever. When something bad happened, my grandmother used to say, 'The Bible says it came to pass. It didn't come to *stay*. It came to *pass*.' I expect Mr. Roland Winters will pass sooner or later."

"He'd better! I couldn't stand to be in the same space with him for very long." Reb suddenly saw his cork go under. As always, he lost his head when he caught a fish. He yelled at the top of his lungs and pulled the fish up.

Wash looked at the catch and grinned. "That's a mighty big yell for a mighty little fish."

Reb took the tiny fish off the hook and then slipped it back into the water. "I can't figure Goél out. Just can't. We're doing pretty well by ourselves, aren't we? I mean, we've never failed him so far. Why does he have to send us 'help'?"

"Don't try to figure Goél out, Reb," Wash said. "It's a waste of time."

When Reb and Wash left camp to go fishing, Josh brought out the swords. It was part of Goél's training plan that they practice every day with all their weapons, including bows, swords, staves, and even knives. They had been through terrible danger too often for anyone to doubt that they might need them at any time.

Now as Josh took out the practice swords—blades blunted and with dull edges—he said, "Jake, you need to work on your swordsmanship a little bit."

"Don't we all?" Jake muttered. "What I need is an AK47 attack rifle." He was impatient with primitive weapons and longed for some of the automatic arms that he had seen before Oldworld blew itself up. He picked up a sword and swished it around. "I'll never be any good with one of these things."

Dave wandered up and heard his remark. "Sure you will. You just have to practice, Jake. Come on. Let's have a go at it."

Jake was still grumbling. "Nobody in this bunch has ever beat you, Dave. Practicing with you is like playing a game you never win."

"Well, you can invent things that I can't." Dave grinned at him encouragingly. His swollen lip was now back to normal. He selected a sword, and the two boys approached each other.

Though all the boys had had quite a bit of practice with blades, Jake was truly bad. On the other hand, Dave was by far the most able swordsman, even as Sarah was by far the best with a bow.

Roland came strolling up and stood with Josh, watching the practice for a while. "I can only hope we don't meet anybody that's got a weapon during this adventure we're going on," he said.

"Why would you say that?" Josh asked him. He knew that some insult was coming.

"Because unless the rest of you can handle a sword better than those two, we're a lost cause."

Dave stepped back, and his face reddened. "Maybe you'd like to try a bout, Roland."

"It wouldn't be fair, Dave. You're just not in my class."

"Oh? Well, maybe you're not as good as you think you are."

"Oh yeah? I'm as good as I think I am."

It looked as if Dave was gritting his teeth. Then he reached for a sword and held it out to Roland Winters, hilt first. "Here. Take this, and let's have a go at it. Let's see how good you are."

Roland shrugged and covered an exaggerated yawn. "Well, all right. I'll use my left hand. That'll give you some break."

"No. Give it your best shot," Dave said. "I want to see how great you really are."

The two boys lifted their swords. Dave, clearly infuriated by the arrogance of Roland Winters, attacked at once. His sword flashed in the sunlight as he put forth his best effort.

Sarah and the other Sleepers drifted up to watch.

Josh saw at once that it was hopeless. Roland lazily parried Dave's every thrust. From time to time he would change his sword to the other hand, and he seemed to be just as good with his left as with his right.

"Wow, he's amphibious!" Josh breathed.

"You don't mean amphibious. You mean ambidextrous," Jake told him. "He can use either hand equally well."

It was obvious that Roland was simply toying with Dave. Finally the stranger parried a blow and in a quick motion brought down his blade on Dave's sword, near the hilt. It tore the sword from Dave's hand.

Instantly the blunted point of Roland's sword was right over Dave's heart. "Well, bout's over," he said.

"That was real good, Roland," Josh said reluctantly. He was very annoyed, but he had learned that he sometimes had to be peacemaker as well as leader. "You must have had a lot of practice."

"Yes. Quite a bit." Roland turned to him. "You want to try it, Josh?" he asked.

At once Josh knew that this was a challenge to his leadership. He also knew that he had no chance whatsoever against Roland. Still, he could not back down, so he said mildly, "I'm not as good as Dave, and I can always use some good advice. Maybe you can give me some."

"Sure. Be glad to help you along, Josh. Come on. Let's see what you've got."

Josh was even more helpless before the flashing blade of Roland Winters than Dave had been. And since Josh was the second best swordsman among the Sleepers, it was obvious that none of them could stand up to this tall boy who cruelly laughed at their weaknesses.

"As I said," Roland commented when their practice bout ended, "I hope we don't meet anything dangerous on this mission. Except for me, there's not a one who could stand up to a really bad situation."

Sarah replied hotly, "Reb here has killed a dragon. How many dragons have you killed, Roland?"

"Never met one. But if I did, I could handle it."

Jake said, "Well, I see there won't be any of the rest of us bragging about anything. You do enough bragging for all of us."

"If you can do it," Roland said coolly, eyeing the small boy with disdain, "it's not bragging. You all need help with any of your other weapons?"

Josh suddenly winked at Sarah. "Maybe you could show us a little bit about how to use a bow."

"Glad to." Roland waved his hand. "Always glad to give advice."

The Sleepers went to the targets that had been set up, and Josh broke out the bows. "Here, Roland, you can take your pick."

"Hm, I've seen better bows. I guess this one will have to do." He strung it easily, something that was very difficult for most of the Sleepers because this was a powerful bow. He made it look so simple.

Roland Winters eyed the target. Then he notched his arrow, and he drew back the string. The motion seemed to be effortless, and Josh remembered how he himself had to struggle to draw that particular bow. He was always just as likely to send the arrow over the trees as into the target.

Roland released the arrow, and it struck the top of the bull's-eye. He turned to Sarah with a challenging smile. "Let's see you kill a dragon, Sarah."

Sarah stepped forward. In one smooth motion she notched an arrow, drew it, and sent it flying. Before it struck, she had notched another. The first arrow hit the center of the target. Before it had stopped quivering, another was right beside it. Four more quickly followed in order. *Plunk, plunk, plunk, plunk.*

Roland gaped at the arrows clustered in a space no larger than his hand. His face grew red. He said, "Not bad."

"No. Not bad," Josh said.

Reb was grinning broadly. "You want to give Sarah a few lessons?"

"I don't need any of your smart talk! Maybe she *can* shoot, but that's not all there is to weapons." Roland turned and stalked off.

"He just can't stand to be beaten, can he?" Abbey said. "What a drip!"

Roland was still off in the grove of trees somewhere when supper time came.

Sarah said, "I don't care if he stays out there all night. He won't like anything we've cooked, anyway."

The Sleepers sat down and plunged into the meal. Actually it was really very good tonight. They had fresh fish, and Reb had insisted on making hush puppies— crisp deep-fried balls of dough. They had onions and garlic and other spices in them.

Wash said, "Mm! Mm! I think the hush puppies are better than the fish!"

"Why do they call them hush puppies, Reb?" Abbey asked curiously.

"Back home, we always had a bunch of dogs crowding around when we were trying to eat. My pap would toss one of these to them when they got too pesky and say, 'Hush, puppy!'"

"That sounds like just another one of your tall tales, Reb." Josh laughed at him. He liked Reb Jackson very much. "Tell us another one of your hunting lies."

But Reb was out of the mood. He had eaten enough for two boys his size, but still there was a frown on his face. Finally he said, "I wish that Roland Winters would get lost in the woods and never come back!"

"That would be a sad thing, Reb."

Everyone jumped to his feet, for there in the open door stood Goél!

Goél entered with a slight smile on his face. He was wearing the same light gray robe that he always wore. The hood that sometimes shaded his face was pushed back. His hair was light brown and had a slight curl to it, and his features were tanned. Sometimes his eyes seemed gray, and at other times there was a blue tinge to them. And just now his eyes seemed happy. "I'm glad to see you all. Sit down, and I'll join you."

"Have some of this fish—and some of Reb's hush puppies."

"I believe I will, Sarah." Goél began to eat hungrily, and he listened as each one spoke.

When all had finished eating, Reb glanced around and said quietly, "Got something to talk to you about, sire."

"And what is that, my son?"

"It's about this guy Roland Winters. He's impossible. Where'd you dredge him up?"

"That's a strange expression—'dredge him up.' As a matter of fact, Reb, his father is one of my best servants."

"Well, his son didn't get any of that," Jake said sourly. "If I ever went on a two-week canoe trip with him, I think one of us would shoot the other."

Goél looked at Jake but said nothing.

Jake's face turned red, and he muttered, "Well, it was just a thought."

"So you're all agreed that Roland is 'impossible'?"

"He's very difficult, sire," Josh said. "No doubt about it. But I'm sure you knew that when you sent him to us."

"I did indeed." Goél leaned forward and put his hands together. He had strong hands, although the fingers were slender. He did not speak for a time but kept looking thoughtfully around the circle. "I understand your problem. He is a difficult young man. But as I indicated, his father is one of the best men that I've ever known. He asked me as a very special favor to see if I could do something to help his son."

"Well, he's a bully and a bragger," Reb complained. "I hope you're not intending to send him with us, Goél. Because I flat out won't go. Not with *him*."

Shocked silence fell over the table. None of the Seven Sleepers had ever downright refused to obey a command of Goél. But Reb's lips tightened, and he sat up straighter. He could be stubborn, Josh knew. For a time Reb's eyes met those of Goél, but then he could not hold Goél's steady gaze, and he bowed his head.

"I will never force anyone to serve me, Reb," Goél said quietly. "If you cannot serve me out of love, it is best that you go and find someone else to serve."

Reb looked up. The words seemed to startle him. And perhaps he saw something in Goél's face that hurt him, for he stammered, "Well . . . well, I didn't mean that I wouldn't do it. I meant that . . . that I don't *want* to do it."

"All of us have to do things we don't want to do, Reb."

"Even you, Goél?"

"Yes. Even me, Reb. But I ask this of you as a favor, and it will not be a command."

At this moment the door opened, and Roland stepped inside. He looked surprised to find Goél there, and some of his self-confident manner left him. "Well, Goél . . ." he said rather haltingly, "I'm . . . I'm glad to see you."

"I'm truly glad to see you, Roland. Have you eaten?"

"No. Not very hungry."

"You'd better try some of these hush puppies. Reb makes the best hush puppies that I've ever tasted, and the fish is delicious."

Roland, however, turned sulky. He shook his head. "Don't care for any."

Goél studied the tall boy for a long moment. Then he looked around the table and said, "I've come to send you on a new mission, my friends. As usual, there is some danger involved, but you have never failed me, and I cannot tell you how proud I am of all of you."

"Can you tell us anything about this mission, sire?" Josh asked.

"Also as usual, I am sending you into a situation where the Dark Lord has gained power. This time he has gained power in very high places. My heart grieves for the people involved, and I'm sure yours will as well."

After talking about the new assignment for some time, Goél took a deep breath and stood to his feet.

"Roland, I have asked you to join with my servants the Seven Sleepers. They are some of the most faithful of all my servants. Now, I must tell you that if you go with them, you will be under the authority of Josh. I have appointed him the leader, and if you cannot obey him, then tell me so at once."

A flush spread over Roland Winters's face, and he glared at Josh.

Josh thought, *He thinks he ought to be the leader. I doubt that he'll go under my authority.*

But for whatever reason, Roland finally nodded. "As you say, Goél."

"Good. Now, we will talk of other things. Later on, I will give you a map. I think you will find that travel to the land where I am sending you this time will be much easier than some journeys in the past."

"I wish we had a coach to ride in. Pulled by six white horses," Abbey said dreamily.

"You will have something better than that, my daughter," Goél promised with a smile.

Roland ate no supper, and he left almost at once.

When he was gone and Sarah had opportunity, she slipped up close to Goél. "Sire," she said, "I don't understand why you want that boy to go with us. He truly *is* impossible!"

"Beyond hope?" Goél suggested.

"Well . . . I don't like to think anyone's beyond hope, sire, but . . ."

Goél put a hand on her shoulder. "There is hope for Roland just as there is hope for you, my daughter. But there is much in him that will have to be purged away. That is the way improvement comes. Everything is burned away except the gold itself." His grip tight-

24

ened on her shoulder, and he smiled as she looked up at him, not fully understanding. "I remember that you had to go through some fires yourself in order to learn. Do you recall?"

"Yes, sire. I remember. It was hard."

"But you have been sweetened by those hard times." His face grew serious, and he said, "Try to be a friend to Roland, Sarah. He needs a friend desperately."

"He doesn't *seem* to need any. He doesn't act like he wants any!"

"But his heart is hungry. No one as arrogant and proud as Roland Winters can be truly happy. So I'm depending on you—and the rest of the Sleepers—to help him." He added thoughtfully, "This will be a double mission. One is to help the people of the land where I will send you, and the other is to help bring Roland Winters out of what he has become so that he will be a good and a faithful servant of mine."

Sarah sighed. "That'll take a miracle, Goél."

"Well," he said, patting her shoulder, "there is precedence for that. Now, do your best, and I will expect to see this 'miracle.'"

3
The Eagles

W e're just going to have to be patient with him."
The Sleepers were gathered about the table for a final breakfast. Goél had disappeared sometime during the night. Roland Winters had eaten his breakfast quickly, then left the house without saying more than a half dozen words.

Sarah looked around at the dissatisfaction on the faces of her friends. "I know he's difficult," she said, "but Goél doesn't do things accidentally. He's sending Roland with us because he has a purpose."

"His purpose seems to be to keep me as mad as a wet hornet," Reb muttered. "Every time that guy Roland says something, mad just goes all over me. I just can't help it."

Wash suddenly reached out and struck Reb lightly on the arm. "You remember when we first came to Nuworld?"

"Sure, I remember."

"You remember how much you didn't like *me?*"

Reb looked uncomfortable. "Well, that was different."

"No, it wasn't," Wash said. "You just plain didn't like me."

"It is too different! You're a nice guy, Wash. I just had to find out about it. But there's nothing nice about Roland Winters."

Josh got into the conversation then. "We're going to have a pretty hard time on this assignment, I think. We always do, but it's going to be even harder if we

27

don't get along. You remember how we've had arguments among ourselves and how tough it was."

"That's right," Jake said. "I guess if I learned to get along with you, Abbey"—here the redhead winked at her and grinned broadly—"I can get along with Roland Winters."

Abbey sniffed. "Doesn't look like he wants to get along with *us*. He won't have anything to do with any of us."

Sarah was uncomfortable with all this. She did not want to repeat her conversation with Goél concerning Roland, but she felt she had to say something to change their thinking.

"You know," she said slowly, "I remember a boy back in the sixth grade. Jimmy. He was the torment of my life—and not just me, either. Everybody else! He was sort of like a Roland shrunk up." Sarah grinned and then sobered again. "I couldn't stand him."

"So what did he do to remind you of our friend Roland?"

"He was always showing off and always bullying kids that were smaller than he was. I thought he was just awful. And I said awful things about him. We all did, but then one day I found out something about his problem. Our teacher took me over to one side and told me things about him that I hadn't known."

"What was that?" Abbey asked.

"She said his father had been killed in the war, and his mother had a terrible disease, and that Jimmy had to do most of the work around the house. I never knew that before." Thoughtfully, Sarah looked out through the window. "When I found that out, I started being nice to him no matter what he said or did to me. And you know what? It worked. He did better. He was really unhappy on the inside, but he didn't want anybody to know about it."

"And you think Roland's like that?" Wash demanded. "Big and tough like he is?"

"I think he may be trying to cover up some things. A wise person told me one time that nobody who's proud and a bully can really be happy."

They sat talking about Roland Winters and his problem—whatever it was—for some time. Finally Josh heaved a big sigh. "I know he'll be hard to get along with, but I'm determined to do the best I can to be a friend to him. He may not want my friendship, but at least I can make the offer." He added, "And now we'd better start getting our gear pulled together."

Goél had told the Sleepers to travel light, so all of them put only what was necessary in their knapsacks. Primarily they carried weapons—bows, arrows, swords, knives—but they also had learned they needed to take along some cooking equipment and weatherproof ponchos.

Goél found them completing preparations. He said, "It is time for you to leave." He glanced at Roland, who had rejoined the group, but did not speak to him directly.

"The enemy on this mission, you must remember, will not primarily be an army," he told them.

"That's good news." Jake sighed with relief. "I'd hate to think we were taking on a whole army."

But Goél's face was very serious. "The greatest enemy this time is pride." After a moment he went on quietly, "You've already learned the dangers that can come from wild beasts and from the swords or the arrows of your enemies in human form. You have practiced hard to deal with this kind of weapon. But there is something just as deadly—in another way—as an arrow in the heart, and that is pride in the heart."

"But I thought it wasn't bad to be proud. I mean, I'm proud to be serving you, Goél," Josh spoke up.

"You're right, my son. Some things we should be proud of. Pride in our country, pride in doing a thing well for the right reason—these are good things. But when one is proud of self and one's accomplishments and one's position, that pride can eat away at a man or a woman—or a boy or girl—until there's nothing noble left. Pride is perhaps the worst crime that a person can commit against himself."

Goél talked at great length about pride. As he finished he said, "I am sending you to a land where pride in the heart of the ruler has almost destroyed that which is good. But it is not too late. He can still be rescued. As I said, you will not overcome wholly by arms but largely through the weapons that touch the heart."

"What are they?" Dave asked, sounding mystified.

"What can touch the heart are things such as love and generosity and consideration and courtesy. Swords destroy, but those things give life. And begin by going to the poor, not to the rich. That is my last word. Now come. It is time."

They put on their knapsacks, and Goél led them away from the house out into an open field.

As they stood waiting and looking around curiously, Josh said, "No horses, Goél?"

"Not this time. Watch." He pointed upward.

Everyone looked toward the empty sky.

Josh squinted upward. He had the best vision of any of the Sleepers and so was the first to see a series of dots against the blue sky. The dots rapidly grew larger, and suddenly he shouted, "It's the eagles! The eagles are coming!"

The giant eagles! On their very first adventure, at a time when it seemed they were all doomed, the mighty eagles—strange mutants of Nuworld, enormous birds big enough to carry a full-grown man—had saved them from death.

The eagles circled above Goél and the Sleepers, their mighty wings outstretched. And then they swooped down and landed. On the back of one eagle sat a small man, who at once slipped to the ground and hurried forward to greet them. "Ah, we meet again," he said.

"*Kybus!*" Josh exclaimed. "It's so good to see you."

Kybus had been the keeper of the eagles. He took pride in them as a man might pride himself in fine horses. He greeted each of the Sleepers and assigned to each of them one of the mighty saddled birds. When he came to Roland, he said, "I have given you the strongest, my friend, for you are the largest. This is Swift Wing."

Roland's face was pale, and fine perspiration stood on his forehead. He glanced at the Sleepers, all excitedly and happily talking. He swallowed hard.

"What's wrong, Roland?" Sarah asked in a worried voice. "You look ill."

"Well, I never feel quite . . . good . . . in high places," he said. "As a matter of fact, heights make me sick."

Sarah put her hand on the tall boy's arm. "It'll be all right, Roland. We've done this before. You'll be perfectly safe. You see, there are harnesses and a kind of special saddle. Once you're in the saddle, you can't fall off."

31

"I guess not," Roland muttered.

Goél had not missed this scene. He stepped closer to say, "Would you rather not go, Roland?"

"I'll go."

"Good. I will tell your father that you are doing well." Then Goél said, "And now it is time for the flight to begin."

The Sleepers mounted the huge birds. Roland watched, then did the same.

Josh fitted himself into the saddle, and the friendly bird looked back at him. Josh stroked the eagle's head, noting the powerful beak. "You could take my head off—" he grinned "—but all I want is a ride."

Goél stood back and called a final word, "Kybus will lead you to your destination. When you are ready to come back, the eagles will bring you."

Kybus gave a cry, and Josh felt the body of his eagle begin to quiver. There was a sudden jolt, and he held on tightly as the bird's pinions started to beat the air. Then the mighty bird took off, and Josh held his breath. Riding an eagle was like nothing else he had ever experienced. He could still remember the thrill that came the first time he had ridden one. Suddenly he shouted, "How about this, Reb? Doesn't this beat a bucking bronco?"

Reb jerked his hat off and, holding to the harness with one hand, swept it around as if he were riding a bucking horse. "Yahoo!" he yelled. "It beats anything!"

Sarah was enjoying the ascent. She was not afraid this time. She knew from experience that the eagle ride was safe enough. Up, up, up, up, the bird under her rose as the earth fell away. And then, at another cry from Kybus, the eagles all wheeled and began a steady flight toward a range of distant mountains.

Sarah's eagle was flying just above and slightly behind Swift Wing. She saw that Roland Winters, for once, was not boasting. In fact, he was clinging to the harness with both hands, and his eyes were shut. Sarah suddenly felt sorry for him. She was not afraid of heights, but at times she had been afraid of close places. She knew what fear was like.

"It's really all right, Roland," she called. "You're safe. And you're doing great. Open your eyes."

But Roland kept his eyes tightly closed. His lips were glued together, and his hands were white as he grasped the harness with all his might.

Jake enjoyed the feel of the wind blowing through his hair. He looked down and could trace the rivers that wound through the countryside below. From time to time the flight of eagles would pass over a village, and the people appeared very small. Sometimes they looked up, and Jake thought, *They probably think we're a flock of ducks.* He saw, however, that some of the sharper-eyed ones were pointing upward, and he could imagine what they must be saying—"Eagles— with *people* riding on them!" He grinned. "That'll shake 'em up a little bit."

Hour after hour the flight went on without a break until, late in the day, Kybus shouted, "There is the kingdom of Falmor!"

Looking ahead, Josh could see a beautiful sight. There was a huge forest, so green it almost hurt his eyes. Sparkling rivers wound between valleys, and he could see the blue of the sky reflected in still ponds and lakes. *It's a beautiful country,* he said to himself. *I never saw any place prettier.*

The eagles began spiraling downward and soon came to rest in an open spot beside a small, quiet river. The Sleepers slid out of their saddles and stretched their legs. Josh noticed that Roland could barely stand up. In fact, he walked for just a few steps, then sat on the ground and stared at the earth without saying a word.

"Thank you, Kybus," Josh said.

"It was my good pleasure, friend Joshua. I will be back when it is time for you to return."

"How will you know when to come for us?"

Kybus grinned crookedly. "Goél will know. He will tell me. Do not fear. The eagles will be here when it is time for you to leave the kingdom of Falmor."

Kybus quickly climbed back onto his eagle. At a word from him, the entire flight rose majestically. Higher and higher the eagles soared. Then as one bird, they all turned in a wheeling motion, their powerful wings beating the air.

Josh saw that all but Roland Winters were watching the mighty birds disappear into the blue sky. "Well," he said to no one in particular, "we're here. It sure beat walking, didn't it?" Then he said soberly, "Now, we can begin our mission."

4

Friends and Enemies

Josh stood studying the map that Goél had given them. "I think we'd better leave the river," he said. He put his finger on the northeast corner. "The palace of King Falmor is up here."

At Josh's side, Roland had been looking at the map, too. "Well, I don't think that's the right thing to do at all." He moved closer to Josh, pushing the younger boy aside with his weight and taking hold of the map. "We can follow the river from here, and it'll be easier traveling."

Josh did not want to argue, but he had had much experience reading maps. He tried to smile. "I know that looks like the easiest way, but walking beside a river is pretty treacherous. We can expect swamps, for one thing, and who knows what would be in them?"

"That's right," Dave agreed quickly. "Nuworld's full of strange creatures. Remember those snake people we met when we first got here?" A shudder went over him. "There might be some of those things around here."

"Nothing to be afraid of," Roland sneered. "I'll lead the way if you're afraid, Josh."

Sarah frowned. "It's not that Josh is afraid, but we've found out that following rivers can be dangerous," she began explaining. "In the first place, they're used for highways—boats and things like that. Until we know what's happening and who our friends are and who our enemies are, it would be best if we go through the forest. That way we can hide until we want to be seen."

"I'm not much of a one for hiding," Roland said.

"You're not much of a one for riding eagles, either, are you!" Reb snapped.

Anger washed across Roland's face, but before he could get out an angry answer, Josh held up his hand. "We'll take the route that leads through the forest. It may be a little bit longer, but I think it'll be safer. Come on, everybody. Let's get started."

Roland Winters grew sullen-faced and flung himself away. As they got under way, Josh led the group, and Roland trailed behind, speaking to no one.

"I didn't handle that very well, Sarah," Josh said.

"Actually, I thought you did very well. I could tell you were angry."

Josh suddenly grinned. "You can always read me pretty good. Even back in Oldworld, first time we ever met. Remember?"

Sarah laughed at the memory. "We didn't have a very good beginning, did we?"

"No. But I thought you were the prettiest girl I ever saw, and I was always scared of pretty girls."

"You didn't show it."

"Well, I just put on. I guess I was afraid of being rejected."

"And there may be some of that in Roland."

"Him? Roland? Afraid of being rejected?" Josh shook his head. "I doubt it. He's too arrogant for that."

Sarah eased the weight of her heavy backpack by putting her thumbs under the straps and lifting it. "That's sometimes just the way. Some of the prettiest girls are very unsure of themselves inside."

"Are you, Sarah?"

"Of course!" she said with surprise. "I thought you would have found me out before now."

They trudged onward, and all the Sleepers began to express amazement at the enormous trees.

"I *never* saw trees this big around," Reb said. "Not even back in Arkansas."

"I think they're a kind of yew tree," Dave said. "They're not very tall, but look at the size of those trunks."

"Lots of game in here, too," Reb said. "I've already seen three deer."

"You did?" Dave sounded surprised. "I didn't see anything."

"They're pretty shy, but I caught glimpses of them. And besides, look at the tracks."

Dave looked down at the ground. No one was the woodsman that Reb was, although Josh thought they all had learned a great deal in Nuworld. But Reb had hunted all of his life back in Oldworld and so was the most expert hunter among them.

They moved along quietly through the forest, everyone's eyes alert. It was just after three o'clock when a deer showed itself, standing on a slight rise.

Roland Winters, who was still saying little to anyone, snatched an arrow from his quiver. He stepped to his right, drew his bow, and released the arrow. It struck the deer, and Roland let out a yell. He ran toward the fallen animal, crying, "I got him!"

All the Sleepers hurried to where he stood over the deer.

"That was a good shot, Roland," Josh said sincerely.

Roland nodded. "This'll put some meat on the table. Reb, I guess you know how to clean a deer. I don't want to get my clothes dirty."

Reb started to protest, but Josh said quickly, "I'll help you, Reb. You're real good at it, and I need to learn."

Reb was still glaring at Roland, but Josh's tone of voice appeared to make him change his mind. "All right," he said.

"Come on, Jake," Wash said. "You and Dave and I can get a fire going and make camp."

It was still rather early for stopping, but by the time they had cleaned the deer and set up camp, the shadows were growing long.

The cooking was simple. They impaled steaks on sticks that they had whittled sharp with their knives, salted them down, and roasted them over the fire.

"I guess I'll elect myself chief hunter around here," Roland said. He had eaten a large steak and now started on another one.

No one spoke for a while. Josh thought that the very presence of Roland made conversation difficult.

But then Josh began to talk about some of their past adventures. But when he mentioned Elmas—the chief interrogator who was the right-hand lieutenant of the Dark Lord—and mentioned the spells that Elmas was able to produce, Roland interrupted.

"Aw, there's nothing to all that."

Josh was offended at being interrupted and especially at being contradicted. "What do you mean, 'nothing to all that'?"

"I mean, there's nothing to magic or spells or any of that stuff."

"You'd better not be so quick to say that, Roland," Sarah said right away. "We've had some experiences that convinced us that truly there *are* dark powers at work in Nuworld."

"Stories like that are just for children," Roland scoffed. He took a bite of steak, then grinned. "The Dark Lord—he's just got all of you scared of nothing! The Dark Lord is just a man like everybody else."

"But he's powerful. And how would you defeat the Dark Lord?" Josh inquired quietly.

"Well, I wouldn't depend on a spell, I'll tell you that." Roland nodded vigorously. "I'll tell you what I believe in. I believe in *me*, Roland Winters! You kids just don't have enough confidence. A lack of self-esteem. That's what some call it. You've got to believe in yourself."

Dave had been studying Roland's face. He said thoughtfully, "Some things are bigger than you are, Roland, believe it or not. There are some things you won't be able to handle on your own."

Roland shrugged his shoulders. "Speak for yourself, Dave."

Roland began to brag then of all the things he had done. He really spoiled the rest of the evening for his companions. The Sleepers had always enjoyed sitting around a fire talking, but the arrogant behavior and the boastful talk of Roland Winters soon wearied them all.

"I'm going down to the creek and fix a trot line," Reb said abruptly. "Catch us some fish for breakfast."

"Guess I'll go with you," Wash said quickly.

"I might as well go, too," Dave said.

And then Jake decided that he wanted to go as well.

Roland found himself alone with just the two girls and Josh. "Guess they can't stand to hear the truth," he said. "What about you, Josh? Are you really scared of this Dark Lord?"

Josh had once been in the clutches of the Sanhedrin and had known the terror of Elmas's dark spells. He had faced death more than once at their hands. He said carefully, "I know there is a power in Nuworld that is not good. And I know I wouldn't trust myself to deal with it. Without the help of Goél, yes, I would be afraid."

"You have to trust in Goél, Roland," Sarah said. "Not in yourself. Goél has strength that somehow he's able to put into his servants. Let me tell you about the time that he saved me from certain death . . ."

Sarah told about the time she had faced death in the Dark Tower. "It was Goél," she said, "who assured me that all would be well. And it was all well, thanks to him."

Roland listened to all this with a superior smile on his face. "I believe they call that self-hypnosis," he said when she finished. "You two can believe whatever you want. Goél seems like a nice enough fellow, but I'm trusting in Roland Winters."

Josh and Sarah exchanged glances.

Later, just before they separated to roll up in their blankets for the night, Sarah said softly, "Don't let Roland get you down, Josh. He just doesn't know."

Josh nodded grimly. "Somehow, I think he's going to have to learn the way all of us did. The hard way."

The next day the Sleepers cooked a quick fish breakfast. Roland Winters did not help. Then everyone packed hastily, and they broke camp.

All morning long the Seven Sleepers and Roland Winters trekked through the forest. More than once Roland tried to change Josh's mind about their route. It was obvious to Josh that, in spite of Goél's warnings, Roland wanted to be the leader himself.

They stopped at noon for a brief break and were

about to eat leftover deer steaks when Roland suddenly jumped to his feet. "There's someone out there," he whispered. He quickly drew an arrow and notched it. "There he is. I think I can get him!"

Josh leaped forward and pulled Roland's arm down.

"What are you doing? You spoiled my aim!" Roland groused.

"Don't be so quick to kill somebody! It may be a friend."

"A friend!" Roland scowled at him. "If they're friends, why don't they show themselves?"

"Maybe they will," Josh said. "Put that bow away."

Several times Josh himself had seen movement among the trees as they were winding through the forest. Nothing was ever very clear, but from time to time he would catch just a flash of something. Now he walked a short distance from the group and stood still, looking intently into the thick trees. He saw nothing, but he was sure that someone was there. Holding up his hand with the palm turned outward, Josh called, "We come in peace. We are the servants of Goél."

For a long moment nothing happened. Then the bushes stirred, and a man appeared. He was brown as a berry, burned from the sun, and wore a short, neat beard. He had on forest green leggings that came down to green leather shoes. A green leather jerkin covered the top of his body, and atop his head sat a pointed cap with a feather rising from it. He carried a bow over his shoulder, a quiver of arrows in his hand, and a sword by his side. But he did not attempt to draw a weapon. The man came closer. "I greet you, strangers," he said. "My name is Goodman."

Relief washed through Josh, for there was honesty

in the man's face and friendliness in his voice. "I am glad to meet you, Goodman. My name is Josh, and these are my companions. We have been sent by Goél to your land."

"I have heard of Goél often." Then Goodman's eyes narrowed, and he asked, "Are you on your way to meet King Falmor?"

Josh did not know exactly how to answer that. "We understand from Goél that your land has some problems. We would like to learn more before we contact anyone," he said. "Perhaps you would eat a meal with us . . ."

"Gladly," Goodman said. "But first, my friends would enjoy meeting you." He put his fingers in his mouth and let out a piercing whistle.

Almost at once the woods came alive. At least twenty men appeared, all clothed in garb identical to their leader's.

Josh blinked. "You are good woodsmen, Goodman, to keep yourselves so well hidden."

"We have to be if we want to keep ourselves alive. We live in this forest, and we are not in favor with the king. But if you would hear more of the kingdom of Falmor, let us have a meal together, as you suggested. We have just killed a wild pig."

The men in green advanced. They were weatherbeaten men, and all were lean and fit.

After Josh had introduced his fellow travelers, Goodman said, "Suppose we roast the pig, and then afterwards we can talk."

"Fine," Josh agreed.

At once the men in green went into action. They soon had a fire going and the pig roasting over it in a most efficient manner.

* * *

Josh soon found that Goodman and the other forest men were very interested in them.

"We do not see many strangers here," Goodman said, as everyone sat near the fire, eating. He took a joint of the pig and bit off a huge mouthful. He talked around it, saying, "As a matter of fact, I might almost say none. The king does not welcome strangers into his land."

"Do you happen to know a man called Bentain?"

"Bentain!" Goodman exclaimed with surprise in his eyes. "Indeed I do, but he is not a member of the royal court. No, indeed."

"He is a good friend of Goél, whom we serve. Could you take us to him?"

"Gladly, gladly. His home is not far from here. After eating, we will take you. And as we travel, you can tell me more about Goél."

The wild pig was strong-tasting, and Roland Winters complained. But Sarah and the other Sleepers had all learned to eat what they had while they could.

Roland was sitting close to Sarah. "How do we know we can trust these fellows?" he muttered.

"Can't you see it in their faces and in their eyes?"

"See what?"

"That they are honest men!"

Roland scowled. "I don't think you can go on that. A fellow can look pretty good on the outside and still be rotten on the inside."

Sarah studied him thoughtfully. "That is true. But after you've served Goél awhile, Roland, you will discover that there's such a thing as . . . well . . . discernment."

"And what's that?"

"It's hard to define. But sometimes you are able to look at a person and just *know* what he's like on the inside."

Roland suddenly grinned. "And what did you just *know* when you first saw me, Sarah?"

So far, Sarah had said nothing at all to Roland by way of criticism. Now, though, she thought it might be well to see if she could help him. So she said, "I saw a young man who is greatly gifted and is unsure of himself and would like to be different."

Roland's eyes flew open. "Well, you sure read me wrong! I don't want to be different. I'm satisfied with myself the way I am."

Sarah said no more, for she saw that he was still stubborn. And she knew that something serious would have to take place before Roland Winters would listen.

Goodman and his band of forest men led the travelers along winding pathways until, perhaps an hour later, they arrived at a small farm. The place was little more than a clearing. There was a small garden, and a few pigs were kept in a pen. Over to one side was a shed where a cow peered out at them, mooing sadly. It was a rundown looking place.

The man who came out to greet them wore a frightened look. "What is it, Goodman? Is it war? Is it the king?"

"No, my friend. I bring some guests. I bring strangers who are seeking Bentain, your father."

Surprise crossed the man's face, and he stood staring.

"This is Garn," Goodman said. "It is his father you seek. Garn, this group comes from the one they call Goél."

44

"Goél!" An older man with a white beard and white hair hurried out of the house. He was small and looked hungry, as did the younger woman and the boy and girl whom Josh could see standing back in the shadows.

"My name is Bentain," he said. "I knew Goél in my younger days."

Joshua felt relieved to hear that. Smiling, he advanced and bowed to the old peasant, who was wearing mostly rags. "I am happy to meet you, Bentain—and your family."

"You bring a message from Goél?"

"Indeed we do. He wishes you well, and he has sent us to see if we can help with the problems in the kingdom of Falmor."

Bentain smiled then. He said, "I will always serve Goél. Many do not know him in this country. Would that he would come and rule over us."

Again Josh was aware of the hunger in the eyes of these people. When Garn said, "We will kill the pig for the evening meal. We have been saving him for such a time as this," Josh knew he must do something.

"No. We will go out ourselves and kill a deer to provide food."

But alarm leaped into Garn's eyes, and he shook his head vigorously. "No! No! That would mean death!"

"Death to kill a deer?" Josh was puzzled. "What do you mean, Garn?"

"All the deer belong to the king," Bentain explained. "Anyone who kills a deer becomes one of The Hunted."

Josh thought this was a peculiar statement. "The Hunted? What does that mean?"

Goodman's face was grim. "Anyone who kills a deer becomes the quarry in the Hunt of Death."

The Sleepers just looked at one another, and it was Roland who finally blurted out, "What in the world is the Hunt of Death?"

Bentain and Goodman exchanged glances.

The man in green said, "As I said, those who kill deer become the quarry—the king hunts them for sport."

"Yes," Bentain said. "That is the Hunt of Death. Many of our people have perished that way."

Joshua's heart sank. If the king used human beings for sport like this, how in the world could he ever be changed?

Bentain said, "Let us sit and talk while food is being prepared. I want to hear more about Goél and his plans."

"Very well," Josh said. "And we thank you. But we will eat only what your family usually eats. Nothing special." He whispered to Sarah, "This is going to be harder than we thought."

"Yes," Sarah whispered back. "I'm afraid so." She shivered. "Imagine hunting human beings for sport. The king must not be just proud. He must be a monster!"

5

The Hunted

I saw poor folks back in Oldworld," Reb muttered to Wash, "but never anything like this!"

Wash looked up at him. "Me either," he said sadly.

The two were sitting by Garn's shed, eating a raw turnip. It was poor eating indeed, but during the days they had been camping in the forest close to the farm, they had discovered that Garn and his family lived on the brink of starvation. There were deer aplenty in the woods, but stark terror leaped into the man's eyes every time one of the Sleepers mentioned shooting one. The family survived on the few vegetables they could raise in their scrawny garden, fish from the small stream nearby, and berries far out in the woods. It was a hard existence. The Sleepers felt great pity for the family of Garn and ate as little as possible themselves.

"I feel sorry for those kids," Wash said. "Robert and Pilar."

Robert was fifteen, and Pilar was twelve. They were small and almost as shy as the deer that inhabited the forest.

Reb glanced over to where the boy and girl were working in the garden. "It would be so easy to go out and shoot a deer for them, but Garn won't hear of it."

"He's as afraid of the king as a man can be. But so is everybody else."

Reb sighed. They had met several of the neighboring farmers and discovered that fear of King Falmor lay over all the land like a cloud.

"Goodman doesn't seem to be too afraid. He and his men kill deer."

Reb said, "But they don't have families to worry about. They're sort of like soldiers in battle, and I guess they're good enough in the woods that the king's men can't catch up with them."

"I know they help the farmers as much as they can. They bring them parts of a deer from time to time," Wash said. "Without that, Garn and his family would probably starve."

Josh and Sarah sat just outside the small hut that Garn's family lived in. They were talking with Bentain and Goodman. It was certainly more pleasant outside than in. The house had a dirt floor and no windows. When she'd first seen the inside, Sarah said to Josh, "We kept our animals better than this back in Oldworld!"

Josh was encouraging the men to talk about their situation. "We won't know how to help unless we know what's going on," he told them.

Bentain spoke first of his relationship with Goél. When Bentain was a young man, Goél had visited this kingdom and had made many friends here.

"So are there many followers of Goél here now?" Sarah asked, leaning forward eagerly.

"There may be, but they keep quiet about it. The king doesn't like to hear about Goél. He has used some of Goél's people in the Hunt of Death."

"That's certainly bad news," Josh said gloomily. "I had hoped that there would be many who would be followers of Goél."

"In the old days there were, but the king himself was different then."

"Different how?" Josh asked.

"He was a good man when he was young, much like his father. Good to everyone. Yes, he was a good king."

"What changed him? He's certainly not a 'good king' now," Josh said.

Bentain slowly rocked back and forth. He stroked his white beard. Then he said quietly, "I think it was the death of the queen that began the change. She died giving birth to their only child, a daughter named Lara. The king went nearly mad with grief. We all loved the queen, and all of us grieved, but King Falmor—I never saw a man carry on so."

"That was probably a sign that he loved her," Sarah said.

"Yes, but he couldn't get over his grief. He began seeing wizards and trying to make contact with her spirit."

"*That's* a bad one," Josh said.

"At the time, I was a good friend of his counselor, Datir. He told the king that he had to learn to deal with his grief and give proper attention to the kingdom. Perhaps seek another wife in time. The king grew furious with him and had him thrown in prison. I believe Datir died there."

"King Falmor doesn't sound like a very reasonable man," Sarah murmured.

"He was once, but no more." A hard light came into Bentain's eyes. "Falmor made a very serious mistake —he began to lean more and more on the advice of a wizard called Zarak. The man gained great power over the king. Those closest to Falmor tried telling him that Zarak was a dangerous man, but the king would not listen. He thought he knew better than his advisers. I believe," Bentain went on quietly, "that the wizard had promised to raise the queen from the dead. At least that was the rumor."

"And the king believed him."

"I think his mind was clouded. Zarak has the ability to cloud the mind. He is Lord Zarak now and far more than a wizard. He is the king's chief counselor. He is at Falmor's right hand constantly."

"What sort of man is this Lord Zarak?"

"A very wealthy man and crueler than you could believe, but the king listens to his every word. As I said, the man is a wizard, and I think the king is somehow under his spell." He looked eagerly at Josh. "That's why I hoped that Goél would come—to break the spell. And something else is most worrisome—Lord Zarak wants to marry Lady Lara. That means that, when the king dies, Zarak will be king over all the land."

Goodman nodded. "It is Zarak who came up with the idea of the Hunt of Death. He thought it was a good way of getting rid of his enemies. All of the king's old and trusted advisers either fled the land or have died in the Hunt of Death. And today, anyone who challenges Zarak's power will die under the spears of the hunters."

"Do you think you can help us?" old Bentain asked, leaning forward pleadingly. "If Goél sent you . . ."

Josh Adams was an honest boy. This seemed to be a hard case indeed, harder than most of their missions. "We would love to help you, Bentain, but it seems to me that more than a war is needed."

"True. True," Goodman said grimly. He fingered the dagger in his belt. "We have a small group of forest men, as you have seen. But my men would be unable to take the king's castle. It is well guarded. And the king keeps a large army to do his bidding."

"Again, true," Bentain said. "They rule the land with an iron fist. It's a cruel world that King Falmor and Lord Zarak have made. This was once a fair land full of love and singing and joy, but now it is like one continual funeral."

Sarah walked down to the stream with a line and some hooks in her hand. She trimmed a sapling, made a pole, and found a likely-looking place on the bank. She soon caught several fish, which pleased her.

And then she looked up. Roland Winters was walking along the stream toward her. He had his bow in his hand and a full quiver of arrows. She thought again what a fine looking boy he was, but she knew it would never do to say so. He was vain enough already!

"Can't you catch anything?" he asked. He threw himself on the bank but laid his bow down carefully. He was very proud of the weapon.

"A few. What have you been doing?"

"I thought I might bring down some squirrels or a rabbit. I'm getting hungry." He looked out through the woods. "I've seen at least a half dozen deer. It would be so easy to shoot one."

"Better not do that."

"That's what everybody says. But why not? The king would never miss *one*."

"From what I hear about the king and Lord Zarak, anyone who kills a deer is executed."

"Oh, sure. In that Hunt of Death. I think that's probably an exaggeration."

"No, I don't think so," Sarah said. "Didn't you see the fear in the eyes of Garn and his family when we even mentioned shooting a deer?"

"Sarah, they are just ignorant people. What do they know?"

Impatiently Sarah turned and faced him. "Aren't you shocked at all over the plight of these people, Roland?"

"There are poor people everywhere. Weren't there poor people where you came from?"

"Yes, and I felt sorry for them. I've gotten to know Pilar a little. She's only twelve years old, but what hope does she have? There's nothing but to grow up in misery and poverty. And Robert, Garn's son—he's fifteen and afraid of his own shadow. These people live horrible lives."

"If you say so," Roland said carelessly. He tossed stones into the stream, one after another.

"Don't you care at all about anybody except yourself, Roland?"

He just grinned at her. "A fellow's got to take care of himself. Didn't you know that, Sarah?"

"I think I've learned something a little better than that. In the first place, most of us *can't* take care of ourselves. We all need help sometimes."

"Well, I don't plan to need help from anybody. Now let's talk about something pleasant."

Sarah saw that trying to reason with Roland Winters was hopeless. He had no idea what it was like to be poor or hungry or weak. He was strong and able and evidently had come from good circumstances. *I might as well talk to that rock about Garn and his family as to Roland*, she thought.

"Maybe we can get us a few squirrels—or maybe some rabbits, at least," Reb said. He kept his eyes on the trees above him, looking for game.

52

"Rabbit stew would taste pretty good," Wash agreed. "There sure are a lot of hungry folks in this country that need to be fed."

The boys hunted for more than two hours but managed to bring down only two rabbits. Reb slumped in discouragement. "If I just had my shotgun and my old dog, Spot, I could fill this sack up with game in no time."

At that moment Wash suddenly straightened, listening. "Hear that? Did you hear that?"

"Hear what?"

"Listen." Wash stood perfectly still, and so did Reb. "That's dogs barking. Sounds like *hunting* dogs. And it's coming from over there. From the other side of that ridge."

"Sure is. Let's go see what it is." Reb took off running.

From the top of the ridge, Reb saw that they were looking down into the valley beyond. The baying of the dogs was growing louder. Suddenly Reb pointed. "Look there, Wash!"

Wash narrowed his eyes and then exclaimed, "That fellow's running away from something!"

Just below them a man crashed through the underbrush. His clothes were torn to tatters, and his face was filled with stark terror. Even as the boys watched, he stumbled into a sapling. The little tree rebounded and threw him to the ground. He struggled to his feet, looked behind him, and then threw himself forward again, ignoring the briars and branches that clawed at him.

"That fellow's in big trouble," Wash said.

Then Reb caught another flash of movement. "Look at what's coming, Wash!" he exclaimed. "Those are hunting dogs! Those *dogs* are what's after that man!"

The baying animals were lean and well fed and fast.

"Those are rough looking dogs. If they catch up with that fellow, he's a goner," Reb muttered. "What's going on?"

"You know what this is, Reb?"

"What?"

"I think it's the Hunt of Death."

Reb blinked. "You reckon that's it? The Hunt of Death?" He kept on watching, horrified. Below them in the valley, the dogs had almost caught up with the fugitive. "They'll get him sure," he said. "Come on, Wash. Let's see if we can help him."

Even as they started to scramble down the incline, the man took refuge on a small rise. The snapping dogs surrounded him, and he beat at them with his bare hands.

Reb caught at Wash's arm, stopping him. "Too late. Look what's coming!" he said and pointed.

A troop of horsemen swept toward the man and the dogs. The riders were shouting and seemed to be having a fine time. Soon Reb could pick up some of what they were saying.

The lead rider was a large man with black hair. He carried a spear. "There he is!" he cried. "We've got him! He's gone to ground!"

Just behind him rode a smaller man, who also carried a spear. "You make the kill, Your Majesty," the smaller man said.

"No. Today it is your turn."

The smaller man bowed in the saddle, then galloped forward. He rode to within throwing distance and with a practiced arm poised his weapon.

"He's going to kill him!" Reb cried. "We've got to help!"

"Too late," Wash said sadly.

Indeed, it was too late.

Unbelievingly, Reb and Wash stared at the sight below.

"Might as well go, Reb," Wash said. "We can't do anything for him now."

The boys fled back through the forest, still horrified at what they had seen. As soon as they ran panting into the camp, they were surrounded by the other Sleepers, who wanted to know what was wrong. Bentain was also there, along with Garn and his family.

Reb could hardly speak, so filled was he with anger. Wash told the story of what they had seen.

Bentain said sadly, "Poor fellow. Poor fellow. Probably one of the farmers from nearby."

Reb said through tight lips, "I've seen some bad things in my time in Nuworld, but that was the worst. What kind of a king is this, anyhow?"

Bentain met his eyes. "He is a proud man who is in the power of the Dark Lord, my friend. Zarak is but the instrument. He has blinded the king's eyes, and unless something happens, we all must die. The land itself will perish."

6
Roland's Mistake

I think what we ought to do is attack the palace."
  The Seven Sleepers were gathered around their campfire on the edge of Garn's farm. They had eked out a meal of squirrel and rabbit, all thrown together into a stew. There had not been enough to go around, but no one complained—this time not even Roland.

  But it was Roland who had spoken. Everyone's eyes turned toward him.

  "Attack the palace!" Josh said in disbelief. "You heard what Goodman said. To do that would take an army."

  "Well, Goodman doesn't know everything," Roland insisted. He looked dirty and uncomfortable and was no doubt hungry. "I say the king doesn't always stay in the palace," he said crossly. "You saw him, didn't you, Reb—when you and Wash were out hunting?"

  "Yes, and he had his guards with him, and they look like rough fellows," Reb answered. "You think you could've done something to save that man if you had been there?"

  Roland glared. "I would have made a try, at least!"

  "Wait a minute, Roland. That's not fair," Abbey said quickly. "You're always jumping to conclusions and thinking you can do things better than anybody else."

  Roland grew angrier. He got to his feet and stood looking down at the Sleepers. "We could stay around here for a year and not get anything done! We'll probably all starve to death in this blasted forest!"

"You don't really think we should attack, do you, Roland?" Josh asked curiously. He was sure that a successful attack was impossible and could not believe that the tall young man was serious. "Attacking would be suicide!"

"I've heard a lot of tales about you Seven Sleepers. Looks like they were all just a lot of hot air."

Jake threw a stick onto the fire and sent the sparks flying upward. Ordinarily he was fairly hot tempered himself, but now he just looked discouraged. He merely said, "Don't you remember what Goél told us, Roland? You must have a short attention span."

"What are you talking about now?" Roland demanded.

"Goél was very clear," Jake said. "He told us that most of the battle wouldn't be a physical one but would take place 'in the spirit.' That's what he said."

"That's right," Wash threw in quickly. "Something's got to happen to change the king's heart."

"Well, one thing would change it—an arrow right through the middle of it," Roland Winters said, and once more he stalked off indignantly.

"I've heard of a pain in the neck, but that guy gives me a pain in my whole body," Reb muttered. "I still can't see why Goél insisted on his coming along."

"Well, his suggestion to attack the castle was sure foolish," Josh said. "No doubt about that. Even Goodman says winning by a direct attack is impossible. And he's lived here all his life."

The Sleepers sat around weary and discouraged until finally it was time to roll themselves into their blankets and go to sleep. Probably none of them would sleep very well.

* * *

When Josh woke up the next morning, he rose stiffly and looked around. Wash and Reb and Jake were still asleep. "So where's our friend Roland?" he asked no one in particular.

Sarah and Abbey had been sleeping in the lean-to that the boys had made for them out of saplings and boughs. It gave the girls some privacy. Sarah came out at once and said, "Maybe he's already gone for a walk."

Josh walked toward her. "Don't think so. I woke up several times during the night," he said. "He just didn't come back."

Sarah frowned worriedly. "You know, Josh, he could have wandered off and gotten lost. That wouldn't be hard to do."

"Maybe so." He gnawed his lip. "Well, we'll have to go looking for him, then. I'll wake up Dave and tell him what we're doing."

Dave took the message glumly. "Just let him stay out there wherever he is," he muttered. "When he's lost, he's not giving us problems."

Sarah said, "We'll be back soon. He can't have gotten far."

As they left the camp, Josh said, "He usually goes down toward the stream when he goes walking. Let's go that way."

They made their way among the trees, calling Roland's name from time to time.

When they reached the brook, Sarah said, "There are fresh footprints, Josh. It looks like he crossed over. They go up to the water, but they don't come back."

The stream was shallow at this point. Josh looked

at it and sighed. "We'll have to go over. He's evidently wandered off someplace. Let's go."

The two started across. The water came up only to their knees in the deepest spot. Most of the time they just stepped from stone to stone until they got to the other side.

"I don't know this part of the woods too well, so we don't dare go far," Josh said.

Sarah agreed.

He led the way, keeping the sun always in the same position over his shoulder. "We don't want to get lost ourselves," he said.

They kept calling loudly. But there was no response, and finally they stopped and just looked at each other.

Sarah said, "Josh, we may be going entirely in the wrong direction. We don't know which way he wandered off."

"I guess so," Josh said. "Well—"

At that moment a frightening man in a suit of chain mail armor burst from the woods in front of them. He wore a strange symbol on his chest, and he held a sword in his hand. "Don't try to run away," he warned. "All right, tie them up."

Four other men stepped out of the bushes.

Sarah looked wildly at Josh, as though she was as stunned as he felt.

"My name is—" Josh began.

"I don't care what your name is. You're strangers. You're probably spies, and you are now prisoners of Lord Zarak."

Josh felt his heart grow cold. Immediately he said, "We mean no harm, sir. We are not spies."

The man strode forward and struck him across the

mouth. "Silence!" he said. "See that their hands are bound securely!"

In moments, Josh found his hands tied so tightly that the circulation was almost cut off.

"They are bound, Sheriff Cranmore."

"Good. We'll see how fast they can run. Now bring out the other one."

Moments later, two more soldiers appeared, each gripping Roland Winters by an arm. He was bound as Josh and Sarah were, and his face bore signs of a battle.

"They jumped me. I didn't have a chance," he groaned.

Sheriff Cranmore pulled a short whip from his belt. He stepped forward and slashed the air viciously with it. "Keep your mouth closed, slave," he said, "or I'll give you something to really cry about! All right, men. Bring the horses!"

Soon the soldiers were mounted, and Cranmore nodded toward one of them. "See how fast you can make them run, Zeiter."

Zeiter was a broad individual with a cruel face. He made his own whip whistle in the air, and he said, "All right, let's see you run!"

The journey was a nightmare. Every time one of the three slowed down, the sheriff or Zeiter or one of the other soldiers struck them across the back of the legs with a whip.

Joshua's blood boiled when one of them struck Sarah. "You're brave men, aren't you?" he said. "Hitting a helpless girl."

Cranmore leaned forward and raised his whip.

Josh managed to turn his face aside, but the whip curled around his neck. The cut stung, but he gritted his teeth, determined not to cry out.

"If you want more of that, just open your mouth, serf! Now run!"

For hours, it seemed, the torment continued. Finally they reached a well-traveled road, and there in the distance arose a castle. They crossed the drawbridge that had been lowered on rattling chains. Josh was almost blind with fatigue.

"Throw them in the dungeon," Sheriff Cranmore ordered. "The lower dungeon." He laughed at their expressions. "You'll have plenty of company there. Lots of rats."

The soldiers seized Roland and hauled him along with Josh and Sarah into the castle and down two flights of stairs. The lower dungeon was a dark place, illuminated only by feeble torches stuck into the walls.

A jailer, fat and greasy, rose to meet them. He grinned and said, "What's this?"

"Spies," was the brief reply.

The jailer opened an iron door. "In there," he commanded.

The three of them were shoved into an evil-smelling cell. A soldier then cut their cords, and they stood rubbing their wrists, trying to restore feeling.

"You'll enjoy your stay here," the jailer said, grinning. "Too late for anything to eat today. Maybe tomorrow you'll get something."

"Can we have some water?" Roland asked.

The jailer grumbled but did bring them a single small pail and a single cup. "There. I don't want to hear anything else out of you. Don't worry about escaping. Nobody ever has."

The door clanged shut, and they all drank thirstily.

"Better not drink it all," Josh said. "We don't know when we'll get more."

Sarah slumped down on some dirty straw and murmured, "I feel like I could sleep forever."

Roland glanced at her, frowning. Then he went to the door and peered through the grate. He saw that guards were on duty in the dimly lit passage. He pulled at the bars on the door, shook his head in despair, and slumped down himself, his back against the cell wall.

Josh seemed totally exhausted. He lay down and appeared to go to sleep at once.

Roland watched them for a while. He had fought hard with the guards, and they had beaten him so that he was black and blue. He was sore in almost every joint. And now as he sat there in the gloomy dungeon with no light except for what came through the grate, he knew fear for the first time in his life. It seemed to grip him like a cold hand.

He stood again and pressed his face against the bars. The fear was almost a physical thing. Suddenly Roland Winters felt completely helpless and alone.

"I hear you made a capture, Lord Zarak."

King Falmor was seated at a massive table. At his right hand sat a young woman, and across from him sat Zarak.

"Yes, my lord," Zarak said. "Three captives, as a matter of fact."

"Who are they?"

Zarak looked at the girl. Lady Lara, princess of Falmor, was eighteen. With black hair and dark blue eyes she resembled her father very much. The emerald-green gown she wore today was trimmed with fur. There was a sparkling ring on her finger, and around her neck was a rope of precious stones that glittered and flashed as she moved.

"More peasants, I suppose," she said carelessly.

The wizard shook his head. He took a sip of wine from a golden cup and shrugged. "Not peasants. They were foreigners, strangers. Spies, no doubt. They'll make good sport at the next Hunt."

"I would like to see them," Lady Lara said.

"See them, my lady?" Lord Zarak lifted his brows in surprise. "Whatever for?"

"I'm just curious. I never see anyone from the other parts of the world. Have them brought in."

"But, my lady—"

"Did you not hear me, Lord Zarak? Are you having trouble with your hearing?"

Zarak swallowed hard. This young girl had often driven him nearly to distraction. Everyone in the kingdom obeyed him and feared him except Lady Lara. But since he hoped to one day marry her and thus gain the kingdom for himself, he forced himself to smile pleasantly. "Of course. Of course. It just never occurred to me that you would be interested, my lady." He raised his voice, saying, "Guard, have the three new prisoners brought in."

Twenty minutes later the door opened, and guards led in the captives.

The guards roughly pushed Sarah and the boys into a room where three people sat at a large table.

She knew at once that the man seated beside the young woman was the king. He had been described by Bentain very accurately. And surely, she guessed, the beautifully dressed girl who looked so much like him was his daughter, the Lady Lara.

"That's close enough. They're dirty," the girl said. She sat staring at the three of them, and her eyes narrowed. "They are not like our people. Where are you from?" she demanded.

Sarah's lips were dry. They had finished off their scanty supply of water and had not been given more. She waited for someone else to answer.

Josh tried to speak for them, but talking seemed difficult for him too. "We are not spies," he managed to say.

"Why do *you* speak? You're but a child," the girl snapped. "You, the tall one. What is your name?"

Roland said hoarsely, "My name is Roland Winters. And we are not spies. We do indeed come in peace." Sarah knew that he had not slept at all the previous night. At the moment he probably could barely see. The bright sunlight streaming through the window appeared to be half blinding him. He blinked at the three figures seated at the table. "We are not spies, Your Majesty," he repeated.

King Falmor fingered the medallion with an eagle carved into it that hung around his neck. He continued to gaze at Roland with a hard light in his eyes. "We've had spies before, have we not, Lord Zarak?"

"Yes, we have, my lord, and these three are certainly not of our people."

"Your Majesty," Josh croaked, "we come in peace. We come from—"

"Keep silent!" the man called Lord Zarak shouted. His face was cold, and his black eyes glinted with an unearthly light. "Take them away. They will be good sport for the Hunt of Death."

"You speak far too quickly, Zarak." The princess lifted her eyebrows and gave the wizard a haughty look.

65

The king glanced at his daughter, and a puzzled expression came over his face. "Why do you speak so, my daughter, and thwart the will of Lord Zarak?"

The princess suddenly rose from her chair. She came gracefully around the table, and the light from the windows falling upon her gown made it sparkle like green diamonds. She halted before the three prisoners and looked them up and down. "There may be some use for them," she said with disdain. "The tall one, for example. My groom is getting old and soon will be unable to attend to my horses. This one will do to clean stables at least."

Roland stiffened and said, "I won't clean stables for anyone!"

Sarah knew that was a mistake.

"Oh? Is that what you believe?" Lady Lara laughed, and for all her beauty there was cruelty in her eyes. "I think you will change your mind. You could not like it all that much in the dungeon. You will like the dungeon even less after a month. The flesh will fall off your bones by then for you'll be fed nothing but a crust of bread and stale water. But the choice is yours. Will you go back to your dungeon and starve, or will you clean my stables and obey my commands?"

Sarah saw that a struggle was going on in Roland. *It's probably the first time he's ever had to take such an order,* she thought. *But he'd better do as she says, or he'll die down in that foul place.*

"Well, what shall it be?" Lady Lara said. "Quickly! Choose!"

Roland Winters bowed stiffly. He might not be accustomed to showing this kind of submission, but the memory of the stench of their foul cell would be very painful for one who had known the outdoors all of

66

his life. To be caged like an animal was no doubt more than he could bear. "I will do as you say."

"You may address me as 'my lady.'"

"Yes, my lady. I will do as you command."

Lady Lara laughed. "I thought you might," she said. "Take him away and clean him up. We'll let him begin by cleaning the stables immediately."

"Yes, Lady Lara." Two guards stepped quickly forward. Gripping Roland by the arms, they drew him outside.

When the door slammed, the king chuckled. "You will have good sport with that one, daughter. He has spirit, I see."

"We shall see if his spirit or mine is the stronger."

Lord Zarak looked unhappy. "He might escape from the stables. Then what?"

"I will be responsible for my servants, Lord Zarak," the princess said coldly.

"And what about these other two?" the king said. "Are they not for the Hunt?"

"I think not, Father. There is work for many slaves in the castle," she said.

"Your Majesty, I protest! To give spies so much freedom—these prisoners could be dangerous!"

But the king chuckled again. "Ah, these two are but children, Zarak. You are too cautious."

Sarah felt a quick wave of relief. At least they were not going to be the quarry in the Hunt of Death.

"Give word to my chamberlain that these are to do his bidding." The king nodded to a guard.

"Let them be given, then, the harshest, dirtiest work possible," Zarak urged.

"As you please, Lord Zarak," the king said carelessly. "Now, my daughter, we shall have our ride together." He nodded to the guard. "Turn the prisoners over to the chamberlain."

"Yes, Your Majesty."

As Sarah and Josh were led out, he whispered to her, "At least we're not going to be hunted down. Not yet anyway."

Sarah could not answer, for the guard jerked her roughly by the arm. "No talking," he said. "You are slaves now. Keep your mouths shut!"

Discouragement swept through Sarah, but she remembered that many times in the past they had endured dark hours. *Goél will not fail us*, she thought. *Somehow we'll endure all of this. Endure and survive.*

7

The Duel

Hurry up! Get a move on!"

Roland Winters felt a stick strike him across the shoulder, and he blazed with anger. He straightened up and whirled, but then he saw the sneer on the face of the soldier guarding him. The man was as broad as a barrel and had huge paws for hands. Roland swallowed hard and nodded without saying a word.

"Go ahead. Why don't you come at me? Try it. Maybe you could put me down." The soldier stood waiting, almost eagerly. "Come on. Take a try. Maybe you can pull my sword out and take off my head."

Roland was strongly tempted to do exactly that, but out of the corner of his eye he saw two other guards loitering in front of the stables. They stood watching with grins on their faces. *Even if I did get this one,* he thought, *those two would be on me before I could get away.* So he simply stood there, quietly waiting.

The guard rapped him sharply on the crown of his head with the stick. The blow stung, and the man laughed. "You're just a real meek pussycat, aren't you? I thought maybe you'd give us a little fun. The last one that tried to get away from here did fairly well. He got out of the castle, but the dogs tracked him down."

Roland continued to stand and wait. He had learned that all the guards liked to poke fun at him. They enjoyed seeing him flare up with anger, and at first he had given them that satisfaction. But he had soon learned better. Now he simply clamped his lips together and stared blankly over the soldier's shoulder.

"Well, you've got no spirit. I can see that." The guard seemed to consider striking him again, but then laughed shortly and turned away. "Clean up the rest of these stables! I want 'em as clean as the princess's rooms. Mind you what I say!"

Wearily Roland began to shovel the muck out of the stables. He had always loved horses and had not minded caring for his own, but there were many stables here and many horses within the stables. He also suspected that the other stable slaves had been moved to other jobs so that he would have to do them all.

"They haven't broken me yet," he muttered under his breath as he filled the wheelbarrow. Then he wheeled the load toward the garden where it would be used for fertilizer. He dumped it onto the pile that he had begun there. Then he straightened up and took a deep breath.

He had been up well before daybreak. The sun was just beginning to rise even now. As usual, his breakfast had been revolting, but he had learned to gulp it down, knowing that he needed the strength it would provide. For a week now he had done nothing but clean stables, and every ounce of fat was pared off him. Because of the hard exercise, though, he had to admit to himself that he was stronger and in better shape than he had ever been before.

Roland's gaze ran around the wall of the castle, and he thought, *There's got to be some way to get out of here!* With a sigh he glanced at the towers that rose high in the air. His eyes took in the ramps where armed guards paced back and forth continually, and doubt and discouragement came over him. Still, though he

70

was not accustomed to being a slave, he had not let what was happening to him break his spirit. He felt good about that.

As he wheeled the empty barrow back to the stable, Roland noticed the Lady Lara coming out of the castle door that led to the royal apartments. He quickly looked down and hurried by, for he disliked having her speak to him. She never failed to make fun of him.

But the king's daughter saw him and stopped abruptly. "You there, slave! Come here!"

With a sigh, Roland set down the wheelbarrow and started toward her. She was wearing a green riding habit, and a small cap was perched on top of her black hair. Her dark blue eyes seemed to sparkle as he approached. But then she held up her hand. "Stop! That's close enough!" she said. "You surely smell worse than the pigs. Don't you ever bathe?"

Roland knew she was well aware that there were no facilities for slaves to bathe. He gritted his teeth and stood waiting, keeping his face as blank as possible.

"Get my horse and saddle her at once."

"Yes, my lady."

He had learned to answer at once and to obey quickly. He walked rapidly into the stable, where he chose the white mare and put a saddle on her. He led the horse out to where Lady Lara stood waiting.

"Well, help me up, you oaf!" she ordered.

He put out one hand to support her and felt the weight of her foot. As he propelled her upward, he was tempted to heave her all the way over the horse, but he managed to restrain himself.

She seated herself and then reached down with her riding crop and tapped him on the cheek. "I understand you are not happy cleaning stables." She waited, but Roland did not say a word. She laughed, then said, "Well, you have learned your place, I see. Get on with your work."

Roland watched her ride away.

At the castle gate, Lord Zarak was waiting for Lady Lara to join him. They rode across the drawbridge, followed by a pack of dogs.

Zarak said, when they had slowed their horses to a mere walk, "You look beautiful today, my lady."

"Thank you, Lord Zarak."

"Do we have to be so formal?" he complained.

She laughed at that. "Certainly. I believe in formality. Oh, and did you happen to see the slave that I've made into my groom?"

Zarak was able to conceal his anger. "Yes. And I still don't trust him."

"He's harmless enough. He will be a good manservant for my father, perhaps, once he learns obedience."

"He'll never learn that. Don't you know that, Lady Lara?"

She gave him a surprised look. "Why?"

"Did you look into his eyes?"

"I don't make it a habit of looking into the eyes of slaves."

"No, and that is the reason you do not know them. If you had been in the world as much as I have, you would learn to recognize rebellion when you see it. I once had a horse," he said, "that behaved very well most of the time. But then suddenly—when he got a chance—he would kick the brains out of any man who came close to him."

"So you think Roland is being a good slave just to get a chance to strike out, or perhaps to escape."

"I know it, my lady!"

"And I think you're wrong. But the next time, Lord Zarak, I shall look deep into his eyes." Her own eyes twinkled. "I'll report to you what I see there. Come, White Cloud, let's go!"

Lord Zarak had to spur to keep up with the king's daughter. She was a wonderful horsewoman.

The guards kept Roland working steadily at cleaning the stables and grooming the horses. From time to time he thought about the two imprisoned Seven Sleepers. He had not had a glimpse of either Josh or Sarah since they were separated, and he wondered what had become of them. But there was no one he could ask. He kept his ears open listening for a reference to them, but none of the soldiers ever spoke of them.

"And what are the *rest* of the Sleepers doing?" he complained under his breath. "The least they could do is try to get us out of here. That's what I'd do if I were out and they were in!"

With one part of his mind Roland knew that this was not so. He knew how virtually impossible it was for the Sleepers and Goodman to stage a successful rescue. The castle was too well guarded. It would take a long siege and a powerful army to bring it down.

The sun was high overhead when the rattle of the chain that lowered the drawbridge caught Roland's attention. He saw Lord Zarak and the Lady Lara ride in across the moat, and he hurried at once to take her horse. At the gate, he reached up to take the bridle, then hesitated.

"Well, help me down, you stupid slave!"

"My hand is dirty, my lady," he said.

Lady Lara sniffed. "I'm wearing gloves. I can throw them away after I've touched you." She took his hand, and he helped her to the ground.

"Thank you for the ride, my lady. It was a pleasure as always," Lord Zarak said. He gave Roland a hard look, then rode away toward the stables where his own mounts were kept.

"Give White Cloud a good rubdown and an extra portion of grain," the princess ordered.

"Yes, my lady."

"After that, I have another job for you." An impish smile turned the corners of her lips upward. "I know you don't take baths, but I do. As soon as you've rubbed down White Cloud, bring hot water to fill my tub. I shall tell the guards you will be coming. The kitchen will furnish the hot water."

"Yes, my lady."

Roland took away the mare and walked her for a time until she cooled down. He was still thinking about Lady Lara's orders as he cared for the horse and whispered in her ear, "If I could just see that gate open for one minute, I'd be on you, White Cloud. And then we'd see if they could catch me."

The mare whinnied and reached over to nibble at his hair.

He smiled and patted her nose. "You're much better tempered than your mistress. I wish she had some of your good nature."

After finishing with the mare, he went to the kitchen. "The Lady Lara says she wants a bath, and that I'm to bring her hot water."

A huge woman with mannish features glared at him. "Well, why don't you get at it, then?"

"I don't know what to do."

"You heat water in that big pot over there. Make sure it's steaming hot. Then you carry it up to her chambers."

"How many does it take to fill up the bath?"

"As many as she says. Now I'd suggest you get started."

Roland built up the fire under the huge pot and waited until the water was hot. He poured it into a large earthen carrying vessel. Then he refilled the pot and put it back over the fire.

The effort to lift the heavy water container to his shoulder made him grunt. Picking it up required all of his strength. He was pleased to think that not many men could have carried it as easily as he did.

Roland asked where the stairs were and made his way up two flights. The steps were steep and treacherous, and he knew that there would be broken bones if he fell.

On the third floor he said to a soldier, "Hot water for the Lady Lara."

"Down the hall—where the guard is standing."

Roland went on down the corridor to where another sour-looking guard faced him. "Lady Lara ordered hot water."

"Stay there. I'll see if you can go in." The guard approached the heavy oak door, spoke to someone inside, and then returned. "In there, fellow," he said.

When Roland carried the water container inside, he was astonished at the luxury he saw. The chamber ceiling was high, and the walls were decorated with beautifully colored tapestries. His gaze fell on one that amazed him. It was at least twenty feet long and twelve feet high. It portrayed a hunt of several men and one woman on horseback. They were chasing a stag. He saw that the woman looked very much like Lady Lara.

"Well, don't stand there! Pour it into the tub!"

Then Roland saw the lady herself standing and watching him. She had changed clothes, and the gown she now wore was light blue. She motioned toward a large, raised marble tub behind purple curtains that were drawn aside. Carefully, he swung the jug from his shoulder and emptied out the steaming water.

"Will that be enough?" he asked politely.

"You didn't address me by my title, slave!"

"Will that be enough water—my lady?"

"Of course not, fool! Fill it up!"

Fill it up! Roland did not answer. He knew that filling that tub would take many trips up and down the stairs. He was sure it would take at least two hours of hard work. However, he tried to let nothing show in his face, and he left at once for the kitchen.

On one of his many trips up and down, he asked a guard, "Don't they usually have several slaves carrying water?"

"They do." The guard grinned. "You must be in favor. She's letting you do it all alone."

Gritting his teeth, Roland went at it. He walked down and back, down and back, time after time.

He became aware of the young female slave who seemed to be attending the Lady Lara. She said nothing to him on most of his trips, but once—when the lady was out of the apartment—she looked around nervously and whispered, "It's very hard, isn't it?"

Surprised, Roland straightened up wearily, his back aching from the carrying.

She was a small girl with chocolate brown eyes and brown hair drawn back in a single braid. She wore a simple gray garment. She whispered, "My name is Bettis."

"And I am Roland."

"Don't be discouraged, Roland," the girl said. "It is hard, indeed, but better things will come for you."

"I don't know why you would think that," Roland said. He was still surprised at her friendliness. "How long have you been a slave here?" he asked curiously.

"All my life. I was taken from my parents when I was only a year old, and I was raised to serve the Lady Lara."

"Well, I can't say much for your mistress. She's as mean as a snake."

The girl's hand flew to her mouth. "Don't say that," she whispered. "Really, she has a good side to her. She's very kind to me—sometimes."

"And very cruel sometimes?"

"She's—she's spoiled, but really she—"

At that moment footsteps sounded, and Lady Lara entered the chamber. "And just what are you two talking about?" she demanded.

"I was wondering if there is enough water in the tub," Roland said quickly. That was true enough, he thought.

"I'll tell you when it's enough!" She walked to the tub and looked in. "Keep bringing water until it's *full*," she said.

Roland knew that the water would be cooling off by now and that this was just her way of tormenting him. He knew better than to say anything, however, and he made more trips.

When the tub was full to the brim, Lady Lara said, "That's enough. You can go now. Come back in an hour, and you can empty the tub and clean it."

"Yes, my lady." Roland ground his teeth, and this time apparently he did not successfully conceal his anger.

Lady Lara moved closer. "Stand still," she said. "Look me in the eye."

Wondering what to expect now, Roland fixed his gaze on her face. She was a beautiful young woman. He had to admit that. But she was also cruel. Besides, he resented being ordered about by anyone.

"I was recently told," Lady Lara mused, "that the eyes give people away." She studied his eyes carefully. "You have strange-colored eyes. They are green. I have never seen eyes quite like that." She waited for him to speak. When he did not, she leaned closer. Then she said, "I was told it is possible to see rebellion and hatred in the eyes of some." She studied him for several moments more, then said, "I think I see it in you."

"And what would you expect from a slave, Lady Lara?"

Apparently stunned at his bold reply, Lady Lara's mouth fell open. "And what do you see in *my* eyes, slave?"

At once, without really thinking, Roland said, "I see a spoiled, cruel young woman who has no thought for anyone but herself."

Lady Lara stiffened, and anger darkened her face. "Get out!" she screamed. "Get out! I don't have to listen to a slave." She was pale with rage.

As he left the room with the empty water container on his shoulder, he could hear Bettis say, "Don't be angry, my lady. He didn't know any better."

"He'll learn to submit!" Lady Lara vowed as the slave Roland closed the great oak door. "He'll learn to submit!" She turned to Bettis. "You heard what he said. It's a lie, isn't it? Isn't it a lie?"

Bettis had learned to be tactful beyond her years. "He just doesn't understand you, my lady. After all, he's just a slave. How could you expect him to?"

"Well, I suppose that's true enough, but he has such an arrogant streak in him!"

Bettis thought but did not speak. *Not as arrogant as yours, Lady Lara.* She changed the subject by saying, "Now will you have your bath?"

On the day following his unpleasant encounter with the Lady Lara, Roland finally had a chance to speak with Sarah and Josh. He had been cleaning the stables again and was wheeling his load out to the garden when he saw the two of them. They were spreading the manure that he had brought the day before. "Josh, Sarah!" he whispered. "Are you all right?"

Both Josh and Sarah turned with surprise. "Roland!" Sarah cried. "We've been worried, wondering what happened to you."

"Nothing really too bad so far," he said. "What about you?" He saw at once that both Sarah and Josh were pale and looked half-starved. "Aren't they feeding you?" he asked.

"Aw, we're all right," Josh said. "The food's terrible, and they work us from dawn until long after dark, but we're all right."

"Me too," Roland said. "What do you think the others are doing? Do you think there might be a rescue attempt?"

"Not a chance," Josh said. "Look at those castle walls."

The three talked while Sarah and Josh raked manure.

But then a guard came along and said, "Get to work, you!" He swished his short whip and struck Roland across the shoulders. "Get back to your work! And you two, let's see that dirt fly!"

There was no more chance to talk with Josh and Sarah, but Roland found himself glad that they were all right. *They're having a rough time,* he thought and was a little surprised at himself. He had never before felt much concern for anyone but Roland Winters.

Later that afternoon, when he was back at grooming the horses, he heard the clanging of swords out in the courtyard. Curious, he decided he would lead Lady Lara's mare to the blacksmith at the far end of the court. Then he could see what was going on.

At once he saw that several officers including Lord Zarak and his henchman Sheriff Cranmore were engaged in sword practice. A small crowd stood watching. He would have passed by, but Lady Lara's voice rang out. "Slave, stop! Where are you going with my horse?"

"She needs a new shoe, my lady. I was taking her to the blacksmith."

"Let me see!"

"It's her right rear hoof, my lady," Roland said. "You can see that part of the shoe is worn off. It's going to make her lame if it's not replaced."

Lady Lara's eyes opened wider. "Well, you do know something about horses after all."

"A little, my lady."

Then there were shouts, and both Roland and the princess turned to see that Sheriff Cranmore had been victorious over one of the soldiers. He had his sword tip pressed against the man's chest.

"Don't kill him, Cranmore," Zarak said, laughing.

"He may be good for something. Maybe for serving in the kitchen."

The sheriff turned away from his defeated foe. He was grinning broadly. "Not much competition around here."

Lady Lara cast a glance at Roland. "You probably never saw anyone who could handle a sword as well as Sheriff Cranmore. You would have no one in your country capable enough to beat him."

An impish impulse came over Roland just then. He knew that everyone was listening, and he said loudly, "Oh, I've seen a few. My younger brother could take him. He would probably carve him up like a turkey."

Sheriff Cranmore's eyes blazed. He came over and put the tip of his sword under Roland's heart. "I'll kill you for that, slave!"

"No, no, Cranmore. Let him fight you!" Lord Zarak said. "That will give you opportunity to carve him up as you please."

Roland saw the swift glance Zarak exchanged with Cranmore. The two understood each other.

"All right," the sheriff agreed. "Give the beggar a sword."

One of the soldiers advanced and handed a sword to Roland, hilt first. The man's expression was not encouraging. He said, "Well, I hope you've had a full life, because it's over now."

Even Lady Lara showed alarm. "You can't fight him!" she cried. "You'll be killed!"

Roland took the sword, hefted it, and tried to hide the light of battle he was sure was in his eyes.

"You can sing at my funeral, Lady Lara," he told her. "I know you'd enjoy that."

A surprised mutter went up from the soldiers, and

Lord Zarak said loudly, "The slave is insolent. Make it short and sweet, Cranmore."

The sheriff laughed and swung his sword in the air. "Come to me, slave!" he said. "Would you rather have my blade in your throat or in your heart?"

"As you please, Sheriff Cranmore," Roland said. What he knew and the others did not know was that all of his life he had practiced with a sword. He had been a champion when he was only sixteen years old and had never been beaten since. He also had seen Cranmore fight and had studied his style. Now he simply stood before the sheriff with his blade half-lifted.

"He doesn't even know how to hold the blade," Cranmore jeered. "Well, this will be a lesson in swordsmanship for you, slave, but you won't stay alive to profit by it."

Lady Lara watched Cranmore spring forward with the clear intention of ending the battle with one swift blow. But the slave's blade flew up, misdirected the sheriff's aim, and the thrust drove by him.

Humiliated by his failure, Cranmore clenched his teeth and began a series of rapid lunges. The ring of steel on steel filled the courtyard, and other servants and soldiers were drawn to the conflict. Many looked down from the windows.

Lady Lara could scarcely believe what she was seeing. She realized that Roland could have killed Cranmore more than once. *I never saw anyone who could handle a sword like that,* she thought. *He is just playing with the man!*

On the sidelines, Lord Zarak was furious. He shouted, "Kill him, Cranmore!"

The sheriff was trying his best. Around and

around the two went. Now Cranmore was breathing hard.

There was a smile on Roland's lips as he easily parried the sheriff's sword thrusts. And then, abruptly, with a strange, twisting movement, he drove forward, and the tip of his blade was inside Cranmore's guard. He wrenched away the sheriff's sword, and it went spinning high into the air. Instantly Roland placed the tip of his blade on Cranmore's throat. "Would you rather have it in the throat or in the heart, my lord?"

"Stop him!" Zarak cried.

Instantly soldiers surrounded Roland and took away his sword.

Zarak shouted, "You'll be executed for this!"

But Lady Lara said, "This is my slave, my lord, and it was your plan that failed. I cannot help it if your underlings are incompetent."

She turned then to Roland. "Come with me, slave. You may take my horse to the blacksmith. Then I have work for you to do."

The crowd watched in silence as Roland went to retrieve the marc and follow her.

When they were out of hearing distance, she said to him, "You are in great danger. Cranmore is a very dangerous man."

"But why should you care?" The exercise and the challenge and the victory had obviously quickened Roland's boldness. "I'm just a slave, and you don't care about slaves."

"That's not true," she protested angrily. "I care for Bettis."

"And what about those that are starving outside this castle? What about the slaves who work here night and day so that you can live in comfort?"

Lady Lara never could stand criticism. She slapped his face. "I'll have you thrown back into the dungeon!" she cried. "You can't talk to me like that!"

"You see? I was right." There was no quieting him. "You don't care for anybody but yourself."

"Guard, put this slave in the dungeon!" she screamed.

Lady Lara watched as he was led away. Oddly, she found herself trembling. She stabled the horse herself and then went to her chamber.

Bettis came to her at once. She was sure the maid had watched the duel from the window.

"What is wrong, my lady?"

"That Roland! That slave! He told me that I didn't care for anybody but myself."

First, it seemed that Bettis was going to keep a tactful silence. But then she simply said, "He is a good man, Lady Lara."

"He is a slave."

"Still, if he were a prince and had come on a powerful warhorse, clothed in armor, would you not look on him with favor?"

Lady Lara stared at the girl. "Well, he's not, and he didn't, and I've had him thrown into the dungeon. He'll learn how to treat me with respect."

8
The Quarry

"All right, you. Come with me."

Startled, Sarah looked up at the tall, forbidding woman who stood before her. It was Dagmar, who was in authority over the slaves that worked in the kitchen.

"Come where?" Sarah asked. She glanced over at Josh, and he appeared to be as startled as she was. The two had been scouring pots and pans, and both were greasy and filthy.

"I don't know what you've done to deserve this honor," the woman sneered, "but Lady Lara's maid is sick. Her command is that you will take her place."

"Me?" The woman's news startled Sarah, but she knew there was no arguing with it.

Dagmar had been cruel to both Sarah and Josh—as she was to the rest of the slaves. Now her muddy brown eyes were filled with unusual hatred. "Come along," she said. "You can't serve her lady stinking like the swine."

Josh nodded, saying, "Go on, Sarah. It'll be better for you than this."

"Silence, slave!" Dagmar cried. "And you, girl, come along."

Dagmar led Sarah to a room just off the kitchen and said, "You've got to be cleaned up. Have you ever had a bath?"

"Yes. Of course, I've had baths."

"Well, don't be so proud of it. There—the water's heated." She pointed to a metal tub. "Get in there and scrub yourself."

What a blessed relief to soak herself clean, Sarah thought. She found that a bar of soft soap had been left for her. She even washed her hair.

And then Dagmar returned with—wonder of wonders—clean underwear, a pair of black shoes, and a simple gray dress. "Put these on," she ordered. She watched as Sarah scrambled into the clothes. Then she commanded, "And do something with your hair!"

There was nothing to do with except a comb and a brush, but Sarah did her best. It felt so good just to be clean again. *Whatever happens to me from now on,* she thought, *I got a bath!*

"All right. All right. You'll have to do. Go up those stairs. Ask the guards to direct you to the lady's rooms. And mind your manners, or she will have the hide taken off your back."

Sarah found her way without difficulty to the chamber of Lady Lara.

The guard gave her a stare, then winked. "You've sure come up in the world now. Better go on in. Her ladyship's been waiting for you."

Sarah entered the door that the guard opened and saw Lady Lara standing by the window, looking out. "They told me to come to you, my lady."

"Yes. My maid's ill. You'll have to serve in her place. You probably don't know anything about waiting on ladies."

"Not a great deal, but I'll do my best, my lady."

"All right. I need to change clothes, and then you must do my hair."

Lady Lara watched her new maid work and was amazed to find that she was very capable indeed. The girl's hands were gentle, and she had a way of arranging hair that pleased the lady very much. "You do well," she said. "As well as Bettis, and she has taken care of me all of her life."

"You have beautiful hair, my lady. Very beautiful, indeed."

For some time Lady Lara simply relaxed. She was highly pleased with all the attention she got and with the quickness of the slave. "What is your name, girl? I forget."

"Sarah, my lady."

"Well, Sarah, how is your other friend doing? What's his name?"

"Josh."

"Yes. Josh. Is he being treated well?"

"No, my lady. I fear not."

Lady Lara had asked the question just out of curiosity. She really had no interest in slaves. She stared at the girl, surprised at her answer. "And you. I suppose you haven't been treated well, either?"

"I do not complain. My lady asked me, and I told you. We've both been half starved and worked until we couldn't stand up."

Lady Lara did not know whether to be angry or not. *However, I did ask the question,* she thought. *I can't get angry with the girl if she gives me an answer. And she is polite enough.*

"Your other friend has been returned to the dungeon. Did you know that?"

"Oh, no. I didn't know. What has he done?"

"He was insolent. To me!"

The hand on Lady Lara's hair seemed to tremble slightly. "I'm truly sorry to hear that, Lady Lara," she said.

"Has he always been as insolent to his betters as he is now?"

"I have not known him very long, my lady."

"Tell me about him."

"What would you like to know, my lady?"

"He puzzles me. He's the best swordsman I've ever seen, and yet he's rebellious and insolent. He can't learn his place."

"Perhaps it would help to understand, Lady Lara," her new maid said quietly, "that he has never been a slave before. He has always been free—indeed, as we all have been. Imagine, if you can, if you yourself suddenly were made a slave. It would be very difficult for you, would it not—my lady?"

Lady Lara was silent. She kept on looking at her reflection in the mirror as the girl arranged her hair. She studied Sarah's face in the glass and saw no insolence there. Then she turned around and looked directly into her eyes. She said, "I don't see any hatred or rebellion in you. But when I look into Roland's eyes, I see anger."

"He is a confused young man, my lady. But he has some fine qualities. He has been spoiled, and that is never good for anyone."

"Spoiled how?"

"In every way, I fear. He comes from a wealthy family, he has always had everything he wanted, and perhaps you have noticed how fine looking he is."

"Why should I notice what a slave looks like?"

"Well, perhaps not. But other girls have found him so. It is impossible that they should not. I myself think he is one of the finest looking boys I've ever seen! Strong, and tall, and that red hair and green eyes!" Sarah went on. "I think he's *very* handsome, my lady."

"Well . . . perhaps if he were cleaned up. Then he might be presentable."

"Yes, my lady."

For some time, Lady Lara asked Sarah questions. She found herself growing very curious, indeed. At last she said, "And what are you three doing here? How did you come to this land, and *why* did you come?"

Somewhat cautiously, Lady Lara thought, Sarah began to speak of their travels and of an unusual person named Goél. She told of the courage and the goodness of Goél and how he had saved her life and the lives of her friends many times.

"I have heard something of this Goél," Lady Lara said. "But I thought he was merely a story made up."

"No, indeed, lady. He's more than that. He is real. If you ever meet him, you will know that there is nobody like him. Nobody at all."

Lady Lara did not talk further about Goél, but as she allowed Sarah to help her dress, she was thinking deeply about what she had just heard.

The cell door suddenly swung open, and Roland blinked in confusion as he was dragged out into the passageway.

"Come along!" the guard said roughly.

"Where are you taking me?"

"Don't ask questions. You will be safer that way."

Roland kept quiet, and the guard guided his steps. After they had made several turns, he was pushed through a door and slammed down into a chair. The room was dark except for a single light that shone into the darkness from above.

"Stay seated. I want to talk to you," someone said from behind him.

Instantly Roland knew that voice. He had heard it often enough to recognize it. The speaker was Lord Zarak. And for some reason, Roland became suddenly afraid. If physical danger were being threatened, he might have faced it with more courage, but there was something evil about this very room.

"You will answer my questions," Zarak said. The king's counselor moved around into Roland's line of vision. He had removed the medallion he always wore and was slowly swinging it to and fro, so that it reflected flashing rays of light. His voice became soft as he began to ask Roland about many things.

There was something about the medallion that Roland could not understand. In the first place, he was unable to take his eyes off it. And as he watched it swing back and forth, back and forth, back and forth, his mind seemed to be grasped in a way that he had never known. The voice of Zarak went on asking questions, asking questions, and Roland had to struggle in order to answer without giving away any important facts.

I can't let Zarak know that there are other Sleepers out in the forest. He would hunt them down.

That was Roland's resolve, but it was very difficult to carry out. He also noticed that a strange incense was burning. The incense, as well as Zarak's voice and the medallion, seemed to paralyze his mind.

And dimly he remembered what he had been told by Josh and the other Sleepers: *There are strange powers at work in this world, and the battle will not be a battle with swords or arrows so much as a battle for the mind. Lord Zarak is powerful in the dark arts. If you ever encounter him, you will have to be able to stand in the spirit.*

On and on the questioning went. By now Roland could barely sit up.

Then he heard Zarak's voice say triumphantly, "There. You see, Your Majesty, he has condemned himself."

Roland had no idea what it was he had said. He still felt half drugged by the sight of the medallion, by the voice of Zarak, and by the smell of the incense. He did manage to look up and see that there was now a third person in the room—King Falmor.

The king stood staring at him strangely. Then Falmor nodded his head. "Yes, I can see that he is a dangerous one. A dangerous one, indeed."

"Then I have your permission to use him in the Hunt of Death?"

"Certainly. We cannot have such dangerous ones among us."

Lady Lara looked up from where she sat on the garden bench to see Lord Zarak coming across the courtyard toward her. The counselor wore an unusually satisfied smile on his face.

"And why are you so happy today, Lord Zarak?" she asked.

"Because I have at last convinced the king concerning your slave."

"Roland? What about Roland? He's in the dungeon."

"Yes, but the king and I have interrogated him, and he has revealed that he is a traitor."

Lady Lara studied the man's face. He was triumphant indeed. And she began to feel a strange sensation. "What—what did my father say?"

"Your father has given orders that your slave will

be the quarry in the next Hunt of Death. You have had your fun tormenting him, but now your father has spoken. He will die under my spear."

The king's daughter could not answer.

She got up at once and went to her chamber, where Sarah took one look at her face and said, "You look troubled, my lady."

"Your friend Roland—he has been condemned to be the quarry in the next Hunt of Death."

"Oh, no!" Sarah cried. "That must not happen! But . . . but why?"

"He is the enemy of my people. Why should I care about a slave?" Lady Lara said, but she walked the floor. "He is the enemy. He must die. Death is the proper sentence for an enemy."

Her maid stood straight and waited until Lady Lara's eyes met hers. Then she said quietly, "He is not your enemy, my lady. He came with all the rest of us to help your people."

Lady Lara hesitated. She could not understand the sensations that were going through her. "Indeed, I wish I could do something," she said finally. "But it is my father's command."

"You are your father's daughter. He will listen to you," Sarah pleaded.

"No, I can do nothing. He is the enemy of our people." Lady Lara repeated this loudly as if to convince herself, and then she said to the girl, "Leave me now!"

"Yes, my lady."

As soon as her maid left the room, Lady Lara threw herself across her bed. She found herself totally unable to explain the feelings that were swirling in her. "Why should I care about him?" she asked aloud. "He is just a slave. Just a slave." But she realized that somehow, in some strange way, the slave Roland Winters had made an impression on her. She lay on the bed for a long time, thinking, searching for a solution.

Then Lady Lara whispered, "No, there is nothing I can do. I cannot change my father's command."

9

The Visitor

Dave and Reb lounged on one side of the campfire, while Abbey and Wash sat on the other. Jake, sitting a little apart from the other Sleepers, picked up a stick and poked at the flames. Sparks flew furiously.

Dave jerked back, yelling, "Watch out! You're sending sparks all over me! You want to set me on fire?"

Jake gave him a short glance and then looked back at his stick. "I don't know what we're going to do," he said. "I sure wish Goél was here."

Goodman and Bentain, who had joined the Sleepers this evening, were sitting a short distance from the fire. When no one else spoke, Goodman said, "I wouldn't have too much hope for your friends if I were you. No one has ever come out of the dungeons— or if they did, they were in pitiful shape."

"But we've got to do something!" Abbey said loudly. "We can't just sit here and not help."

"Abbey's right," Reb agreed. "Look, Dave. You remember that time we were all mixed up with that wizard's castle in Whiteland and you scaled the wall? Why couldn't you do that again?"

"I probably could," Dave said. "But what would I do when I got inside?"

"Why, you could knock out the guards, lower the drawbridge, and then we'd come charging in."

"That is not a good plan," Goodman said quickly. "The inside of that castle is swarming with guards. It would be like stepping on an anthill. Day or night."

Silence fell over the group. The fire hissed. A log settled, sending more sparks flying upward.

"I know you came to help, my friends," Goodman said sympathetically, "and you have been disappointed. But all is not yet lost."

At that moment old Bentain got to his feet. "Goodman is right," he said. "It is never a good time to give up. As long as we are alive, we have hope. As long as we have hope, we are alive. But when hope is gone, we might as well jump into a hole and pull it in after us, as the ancient saying goes."

"Do you have any ideas, Bentain?" Dave asked.

"I have one."

"Well, let's have it," Reb said. "Whatever it is, it'll be better than anything I've got."

"I have been thinking much about this. Goél sent you young people to this place. I believe that he knows what is going on. We know that the king is not going to free your friends, so I think we had better get prepared —even if we don't know what we are preparing for."

"I'm for that!" Reb exclaimed enthusiastically. He was an excitable boy anyway, always unable to sit still. "Goodman, how many men can you raise?"

"As far as good hard-fighting men are concerned— maybe a hundred. Of course, there are farmers around who would probably join us if they saw any hope, but they are much discouraged. We can't count on much help from them."

"Then let's get ourselves ready. Why don't you call all your men together? We'll gather every weapon we can lay our hands on. And then, when the break comes, we'll be ready for it."

"Sounds good to me, Reb," Wash said. "I'm going crazy just sitting around here doing nothing."

"All right, I will," Goodman said with determination. He stood, and his glance went around the Sleepers. "I don't know Goél, but you have made me believe in him. I'll try to put that same confidence into my men." He turned and walked off into the darkness without another word.

"I wish I could be as quiet as he is in the woods," Dave said enviously. "Well, anyway, we'll be doing something."

"What's the matter, daughter? You seem troubled today."

Lady Lara looked up at the king. She was sitting on the marble bench in the garden. The birds sang in the tree above them, and hummingbirds were coming and going to the large purple blossoms of a nearby trumpet vine. She shifted uneasily. "What makes you think something's wrong, Father?"

King Falmor sat on the bench beside his daughter. He put out a hand and touched her hair. "I wish you looked like your mother instead of like me. I've always wished that." He smiled sadly, saying, "If you did, I'd always be able to see her every time I look at you."

Lara was surprised. Such gentleness in her father was unusual. He usually seemed preoccupied with his responsibilities, and she had grown up getting affection from him only at odd moments. In fact, much of the time he seemed completely under the sway of some dark shadow that hung over him.

"I want to ask you something, Father. What was it like when Mother was alive?"

"What was it like!" the king exclaimed. His eyes looked off into the distance. "Everything seemed good and lovely then. She made everything about her lovely, Lara."

Lady Lara thought about this. Then she said gently, "I think she would not like some of the things that are going on today, Father."

The king turned his eyes back to her, puzzled. "What things?"

"The way we live. You—you're so *gloomy*, Father."

"Gloomy! Me?"

"You just don't seem to have any real happiness. I know you miss Mother, but it's been so many years now. Why, you could have married again. You still could. I would not object."

"I could never do that!"

"Why do you say that? Mother was a wonderful woman, but she's gone now. And you're lonely."

"Oh, I have many things to keep me occupied. There is riding and hawking and hunting—"

"Have you ever thought," Lara asked cautiously, "that perhaps we don't pay enough attention to what's happening to our people?"

"Now, daughter, you know that Lord Zarak takes care of all of that. He's a good administrator."

"I suppose, if you say so. But I have been thinking on it, and there are so many *poor* people, Father. They're hungry, and they're forbidden to hunt the deer that so freely roam the forest."

"The deer are the king's property! They are for sport only."

"But, Father, if the people are hungry, isn't it more important that they have something to eat than that you and Lord Zarak and his men have sport?"

The king frowned. "I've never heard you talk like this before."

"I've been thinking a lot, Father. And one thing I know—from what you tell me of my mother and from what others say about her—she would have hated the Hunt of Death."

"You cannot know what your mother would have thought."

"You've always said she was a gentle woman with a great deal of love."

"That she was. That she was."

"Then how can you think she would have liked to see some poor man hunted to death and speared as if he were an animal? You know she would have hated it, don't you, Father?"

King Falmor stroked his chin, and he looked disturbed. "I don't know," he muttered after a while. "The Hunt wasn't planned. It just . . . sort of started."

"And we know who started it, don't we? Lord Zarak! And if Mother were alive, I'm sure she would have protested."

The king got to his feet and paced back and forth, as if what she said had stirred something within him. Suddenly he said, "But why do you talk to me like this, daughter? And why do you talk in this way about Lord Zarak? He expects to marry you one day."

"I'll never marry Lord Zarak, Father! Never!"

The vehemence of his daughter's reply brought King Falmor up short. He stopped his pacing and turned around. "You have never said anything like this before."

"I have never trusted him," she said flatly. "He is a cruel man. If he is cruel to serfs, he will be cruel to his wife. And I'm not certain he is a good man to rule over the kingdom. You are the king, Father, and yet you let such a man as he have so much authority."

"He is an efficient man!"

"He may be efficient, but starving people aren't happy." Lara found herself saying things that indeed she had never said before. "And when you have unhappy subjects," she finished, "that is not good. Tell me, Father, how did the people react when you first became king and you and mother married?"

A happy light came into the king's eyes. "They cheered us everywhere we went. They were filled with love for us. I remember it well."

"And what do they do now?" She waited for him to answer, but he lowered his head. "They flee from you whenever they can, don't they?" When he still did not answer, she said, "They have become afraid of you. That's why. And it is Lord Zarak who has made you an object of fear to the very people who ought to love you."

The king's face turned pale, and he began walking away. He was obviously shaken by the conversation and wanted to hear no more.

But Lara ran after him. Seizing his arm, she planted herself in front of him. "Father, I want you to release Roland from the Hunt of Death."

"Roland the slave?"

"Yes. Roland. He's done absolutely nothing wrong."

"Why, he's proven himself to be a traitor."

"Give me one bit of evidence that he is a traitor, Father. Just one."

The king searched his mind. "Zarak said—"

"You see, Father? 'Zarak said—' You're not thinking for yourself. That terrible man has some kind of *power* over you."

"You must not talk like this!" the king cried. "I don't want to hear it!" He went around her and almost ran toward the castle.

Lady Lara looked after him sadly. *There's no point in trying to talk him into releasing Roland,* she thought. *No point at all.*

The rest of the day, Lara stayed in her rooms and thought about her father. She also thought about herself. It was a time of self-searching. She thought of how revolting she found the whole idea of hunting human beings. *So why didn't I ever say anything before?* she asked herself. And she knew it was because she had been too self-centered.

Finally she straightened, and her lips grew tight with determination. *I'm going to see Roland.* And she swept out of her chamber.

When the princess reached the lower dungeon area, the startled guard stammered, "L—Lady Lara!"

"Out of the way! I want to visit the prisoner Roland."

"But, my lady, no visitors are ever allowed in the lower dungeon!"

"Do you want me to report to my father that you have disobeyed me? Perhaps you will be the quarry in the next Hunt of Death."

"No—no, my lady! Come. I will take you to him."

Roland heard footsteps in the passage outside his cell, and he got to his feet. This was odd. It was not time for them to bring food or the smelly, lukewarm water.

Then the door opened, and he shielded his eyes against the light of a torch.

"Come out, fellow!" the guard ordered.

Roland stumbled into the passageway. His legs were stiff. He blinked owlishly and managed to see a form before him. But he could not believe what he was seeing. "L–Lady Lara!" he stammered.

"Yes, Roland." Lady Lara turned to the guard. "Leave us alone!"

The guard planted his torch in a wall bracket and walked away.

She waited until he was out of hearing and then moved closer. "I'm sorry to find you like this, Roland."

Roland still could not believe what he was seeing or hearing. He stared into the face of the princess but saw no mockery there. He could only shake his head. "I can't believe that you would care how you found me."

"I–I can't, either. But it seems I do. Ever since I've known you I've been . . ."

"You've been what?" he asked, when she did not finish.

"I've–I've been thinking. I've always been especially catered to. Perhaps all princesses are. But I grew up with little direction and with getting anything I wanted. I've been talking to your friend Sarah, and she has told me much about the Sleepers and about you—and about Goél. And I have been thinking . . ."

Roland straightened up with interest. "I can tell you this, Lady Lara. One day Goél will come to this land, and when that day comes, he will make this kingdom a lot different."

"Do you really think so?"

"I have not known him long, but my father has. My father says that Goél never fails to set wrongs right wherever he goes. He has a plan for this kingdom, and he has sent us to your land as part of that plan."

"Roland, you've got to get away from here. They are planning to make you the quarry in the Hunt of Death tomorrow."

"How can I escape?" he asked. "If I try to walk out that door, they will kill me on the spot."

"Not if I go with you."

Roland blinked with surprise. "That's a kind heart speaking, Lady Lara," he said slowly. He studied her face again and realized that something was different. "Someone told me once that, deep down, there was kindness in you. I didn't believe it at the time, but I do now."

She bowed her head and said nothing.

He said, "But I can't escape. I'd have to get past twenty guards, all of them armed."

"But they would listen to me!"

"I do not think so. I fear they would send for Lord Zarak at once. They're all loyal to him. And then you know what would happen."

She stood silent in the dungeon passageway. He could tell that she knew this in her heart.

"I'm so sorry, Roland," she said quietly. "I'll go to my father again. I'll get down on my knees and beg him to let you go." She took a step forward suddenly and put out her hands.

He took them and said huskily, "Princess, you're not the girl I thought you were. You are much more."

She looked straight into his eyes. "And once I saw rebellion in your eyes, but now I see only strength," she murmured. She stood for a moment, then turned away. "I will go to my father. Maybe this time he will listen."

She left him then, and the guard came back. "Back into the cell, fellow. Your last night on earth is coming up. No one ever escapes from the hunters." The man laughed harshly and shoved Roland into the cell.

The door clanked, and the darkness set in again.

10
The Promise

Roland came out of a deep sleep instantly. Fear shot through him, and he sat up, bracing his back against the cell wall. Only a pale light came through the grate of his dungeon door, just enough for the guards to see through. But his eyes were accustomed to the darkness, and shock ran over him when he saw a figure standing in the cell.

He came to his feet in a wild scramble, putting up his hands in a defensive position. "Who are you?" he cried hoarsely. "What do you want?"

"As for your first question"—the man's voice was calm and somehow soothing—"I am Goél."

Astonishment and relief washed over Roland. His knees felt weak. He lowered his hands and took a step back. "Goél," he whispered. "You're really here."

Goél came closer, and the faint, flickering light from the torch outside fell on his face. His hood was pushed back, and his face was lean and sculptured. His eyes were deep set, and they gleamed as he said, "As for your second question, I cannot answer that until I have asked *you* a question, my son."

"You want to ask me a question?"

"Yes, sooner or later I have to ask this question of everyone. All of the Sleepers have had to answer it." Goél stood quiet for a moment, and then a smile touched his lips. "In fact, some of the Seven Sleepers were in a dungeon themselves when I asked it. Some of them, also, were facing death."

"What is the question? Ask it." Then Roland's shoulders slumped. "I'm not sure I can answer it, though. I don't seem to be very quick-witted right now —not with the Hunt of Death hanging over my head."

"This is a difficult time for you, Roland. I know how hard it has been."

Roland still wondered if he was dreaming this conversation. He felt as if what was happening was real— and yet not real. His ears seemed to ring, and Goél's voice seemed to come from far away, clear but distant. He ran a hand through his hair and could only say, "I seem to have been here for years instead of days. I can't believe—"

"You can't believe what?"

"I can't believe how arrogant I was!" Roland heard himself saying. He attempted to smile, but it was a poor attempt. "Being a slave knocks a little of the arrogance out of you."

"I think most men and women go through something like this at one time or another. Those who do not are but few."

"I've had nothing to do but think since I was put in here, facing death. I've thought about my parents. I've thought about how I treated them." He sighed. "What a terrible time I gave them."

"Your parents love you, Roland. They asked me to do something that would bring out the potential for good they knew was in you."

"Potential for good! I don't know how they saw any."

Goél smiled again faintly. "Fathers and mothers have a way of looking beneath the surface."

Silence fell over the cell. Finally Roland lifted his head and asked, "So what is the question, sire?"

"The question is in two parts. First, are you tired of the life you've been living—of being the boy you have been? The second part is, are you ready to follow me and become a different person?"

Roland did not answer at once. He was thinking of his past life. At last he said with sadness, "No, I don't want to be what I have been—ever again. As to the second question, I listened to my parents speak of you for years. I listened, but I *didn't* listen—if you know what I mean." He suddenly knelt before Goél, his head bowed. "If you will have me, I will serve you the best I can for whatever time I have left."

Roland felt two hands upon his head, and Goél whispered words especially meaningful for him. A warm feeling of joy came over him, and his heart seemed to bubble over.

While he was still on his knees, he heard the voice of Goél say, "Tomorrow you will have a chance to prove your loyalty and your faith. They will come for you, and no man has ever escaped the sad result of the Hunt of Death. But I am giving you my word that I will be beside you, and you need not fear—no matter what happens. All will be well."

Then the voice faded away, and Roland's visitor was gone.

Roland felt for the hay and lay down on it in a dreamy state, thinking over and over again of Goél's words. And then he heard himself saying aloud, "I won't doubt you, Goél. No matter what happens!"

The next sound that he heard was that of the rumbling voices of guards outside. He always heard them early every morning when the guard changed. Then he remembered. He sat up straight and looked wildly around the dim cell, almost expecting to see Goél. But no one was there.

"It must have been all a dream!" he exclaimed. He stood to his feet and closed his eyes, thinking. He discovered, to his surprise, that he could remember it all. Roland *never* remembered dreams, but the memory of this one was as clear as if it were happening over again before his eyes.

He heard the guards laughing. One shoved his face up to the grate and said cheerfully, "Last day on earth! Enjoy yourself!" The door opened then, and stale bread and a bowl of stew was set down with a clatter on the stone floor. "Last meal!" the guard jeered.

And then the door clanged shut, leaving Roland Winters alone with only the memory of a dream.

11
Lord Zarak's Order

Lady Lara slept very little the night before the Hunt of Death. She rose early in the morning, tired and depressed, and noticed that her maid had deep circles under her eyes.

"You didn't sleep, Sarah, did you?"

"No. Nor did you."

Lady Lara usually was very careful about her dress, but today when Sarah asked what she wished to wear, she said, "It doesn't matter."

She sat down and motioned Sarah to do the same. For a time, the princess and her maid just looked at each other. Then Lara said, "I have decided to ride beside my father in the Hunt. I have not been able to persuade him to call it off."

Immediately Sarah sat up straight. "My lady, then would it be possible for me to ride beside you? As your attendant?"

"Why, I suppose so—although Bettis would never ask such a thing. Why? Why would you want to do that?"

"I really don't know, my lady. It's just that I am interested in my friend, and I think I need to be there. And I wish Josh could go as well. Would that be possible?"

"I suppose that would be possible. He could help with the dogs."

Sarah brightened. She said quickly, "We Sleepers have been in situations like this before when all looked hopeless. But it is never hopeless, my lady."

"It seems so to me," Lara said sadly. "If my father would only listen . . ."

"Go to him again, my lady. Perhaps he will."

Lady Lara stood, her mind made up. "Help me to dress!" she said firmly. "I shall order horses to be made ready for us in case they are needed. But then I will try to change my father's mind."

Reb Jackson was tramping through the forest with a sack over his shoulder. It was heavy with the squirrels he had killed for supper. He was still not as good with a bow as Sarah was, and he had trapped them with snares.

Suddenly a figure was standing in his path, and Reb's eyes flew open. "Goél!" he cried

"You are surprised to see me, my son."

"I'm *glad* to see you. So will everyone else be. Have you got something for us to do to help our friends?"

"Indeed I have. But first we must arouse the others."

Fifteen minutes later, the Sleepers, Goodman, and Bentain were all anxiously surrounding Goél.

"This waiting has been difficult for you," Goél said, "but now the time has come for action."

"Give me a command, master," Goodman cried eagerly.

"I will. Call all of your men together. Have them come fully armed and meet here as quickly as you can gather them."

"I go at once, sire."

As soon as Goodman was gone, Bentain stepped forward. He was old and bent, and his hair was white, but his eyes were bright. "Is it a battle then, Goél?"

"Most battles that are important are battles of the

spirit, as you well know, my friend. But this time, at least for now, there will be a physical battle to fight."

Bentain smiled. "And I will go with the warriors into battle."

"Your courage has never been doubted, Bentain," Goél said in a kindly fashion. "But perhaps it would be well to leave this to the younger men. Do you not think so?"

For once Bentain argued with Goél's suggestion. "No, sire. I am old, and if I can fight one more battle for you, I will die happy. I will serve Goél until I die."

A cheer went around, and Goél put his arm across the old man's shoulder. "Very well, then, my friend. I would that all of my servants were as eager to follow me as you are. Now—" he looked about at the group "—all of you get ready for battle."

The king heard a knock at the door of his private chambers. He looked up with surprise as his daughter entered. Her face wore a troubled look.

"Lara, what is it?" he asked.

"I must speak with you, Father." She glanced over her shoulder and said, "Wait in the hall, Sarah." Then she closed the door.

"What is it, my child?" The king motioned her to a chair, but she stood facing him. He studied her face and realized that she was troubled indeed. "Are you ill?"

"I must talk with you, Father, and you must forgive me because I have to say some hard things."

The king remained silent. He knew that his daughter had been somehow changing recently and had wondered at the change. "Speak on, daughter. Have I failed you in some way?"

111

"I think you have failed yourself, Father."

"Failed myself! What can you mean?"

"I mean that for many years now you have grieved for my mother. That everyone understands. But it has been unmanly grief for you to ignore the kingdom and your people's needs."

The king dropped his gaze. He well knew that there was truth in his daughter's words. "When your mother died, I was like a madman," he muttered. "I could not find my way out of my grief."

"I know that, Father. I know that. You loved her greatly. You've told me so often, but in losing yourself in your grief, the kingdom has fallen on evil times."

"But Lord Zarak—"

"Lord Zarak is a cruel, wicked man who has somehow managed to cloud your mind!" Lara said firmly. "You must do something about him. He is no fit man to have authority in this kingdom! How could you let such a man rule in your place, Father? *You* are the king! *You* should have seen to your subjects!"

"But when Zarak counsels with me, he gives me some relief from my sorrow," King Falmor protested. "When we meet together, he has an incense that he burns. And he talks soothingly to me, and it numbs my sorrows . . ."

"He has also numbed your kingly aspects, Father. I do believe he has cast a spell over you. Can you not see that?"

"Well . . . perhaps . . . perhaps so," the king said uncertainly. "Very well. I will meet with him no more. Does that please you?"

"And remove him from his place of authority. And, Father, call off the Hunt of Death! It is the cruelest thing Lord Zarak has brought about."

"It is true that the Hunt was Lord Zarak's doing . . ." Then he said, "Still, you are right. I am the king. I should not have listened to him."

"Then stop this Hunt today!" Lady Lara cried. "Now! Do not let it take place."

"Perhaps so. Perhaps so . . ." He looked at her curiously. "This slave—Roland. You seem especially interested in him."

Lara flushed. "He is a human being, and he has fine qualities, and we have treated him shamefully."

"I see," the king said, and he thought he did. Then he drew himself up to his full height. "Very well, I will give orders to stop the Hunt."

He strode to the window and looked down to where Zarak and the lords sat on their horses, waiting. The dogs were yapping eagerly. Over to one side he could see the captive, Roland. Even the serfs who worked in the garden were leaning on their tools and wheelbarrows, waiting for the Hunt to begin.

"Lord Zarak!" the king called down to his counselor.

Zarak looked up with surprise. "We await Your Majesty's presence. It is time for the Hunt of Death to begin!"

"There will be no Hunt of Death!" the king replied. "Take the prisoner back to his cell. And, Lord Zarak, come to my chambers at once. We have things to talk about." King Falmor turned from the window. "Why, I believe I am myself again, daughter." He took a deep breath. "Somehow I've known for years that I have not been acting like a king, but I will do so now."

Down in the courtyard, Lord Zarak's face was pale with anger. He gritted his teeth, then shouted, "Loose the prisoner! Start the Hunt!"

113

"But, my lord," Sheriff Cranmore said nervously, "the king said—"

"The king is ill. He knows not what he says. I will deal with him when we get back." He rode over to where Roland stood, and he lifted his spear. "Run, you vermin, or I will kill you even now!"

Roland knew death when he saw it, and he saw it in Zarak's eyes. He fled across the courtyard, across the drawbridge, and down the road that circled the castle.

Sarah stood waiting in the hall, as Lady Lara had instructed her.

Then the chamber door opened, and the king himself started out into the corridor. However, he immediately stopped in the doorway and seemed to be listening. "What is that *noise?* I canceled the Hunt," he said, sounding puzzled. He hurried back into the room.

Quickly Sarah moved to where she could see him. He was at the window, leaning out.

"What is going on down there?"

From below one of the soldiers, probably, called up to him, "Lord Zarak has commanded that the Hunt begin, Your Majesty."

King Falmor turned back from the window. Astonishment, then anger, darkened his face. "So. Now I see what Zarak is! He is a traitor himself, and I will deal with him."

The king hurried past Sarah, down the corridor and down the stairs. Lady Lara and Sarah followed close behind.

"Bring my horse over here!" Falmor ordered.

As he swung into the saddle, Lady Lara reached for the bridle of her waiting mare. "I'm coming with you, Father."

"Come, then!" And he spurred his mount forward.

Sarah leaped into the saddle of the horse that had been readied for her. Quickly she reined him past the garden. "Come on, Josh! We're going, too."

Without hesitating, Josh sprang up behind her. "What's happening? What's with the king?" he asked as they pounded over the drawbridge.

"I don't know. But one thing is clear—he's not Lord Zarak's man anymore."

12

The Battle

Roland's feet flew. The road that ran alongside the castle turned east into the forest, and he thought, *I've got to get into the deep woods at once.*

When he had gone no more than two hundred yards, he heard Lord Zarak's cry, "After him!" At once Roland turned and darted into the forest. He sought the densest part, knowing that the thick trees would make it difficult for the horses to follow. His greatest fear was the dogs. But he had a brief plan in mind.

The stream, he thought. *I've got to get in the stream!*

The brook that curled around the castle and then made its way into the depths of the forest was shallow during the dry season of the year. It would be no more than inches deep except for a few deeper pools. By the time Roland reached it, he could hear the barking of the dogs.

He plunged into the stream, crossed it, and then cut back into the water. *The water will kill any scent, and they won't know whether I've gone upstream or downstream. They'll have to check both ways.*

He splashed along, making sure that his feet did not touch the bank. He listened to the dogs, hoping that the barking would fade. If so, that would tell him that they had gone the other way. But instead, their baying grew stronger. "They've taken this direction, all right. But they can't track me through water," he encouraged himself.

117

He remembered his dream of—or, perhaps, his actual visit with—Goél. *I promise to believe in you no matter what happens, Goél*, he thought. *So whatever comes next, I'm trusting you.* And he remembered that he had a long way to go.

For what felt like miles, Roland splashed through the brook. He could no longer hear the dogs. They were behind somewhere, searching for a trail. Then the stream became a pool so deep that he could no longer run in it. But it was probably safe to leave the creek now and plunge into the wilderness itself, he reasoned. He tried to get his bearings. *I think I'd better go this way. Seems that the woods are thicker in this direction.*

Briars caught at his feet and tore his clothes as he pushed along. He was weakened by his days in the dungeon without good food, and his breath was labored. An open branch caught him across the face and made his eye burn, but he ignored it.

Roland never knew how far he had run when he threw himself down on a grassy spot to rest. His breath came in sobs. He had no idea where he was. *For all I know*, he thought, *I may be going around in circles. But at least I still don't hear the dogs.*

When he had caught his breath, he tried to take a bearing on the sun. It was going down rapidly. The huge trees around him now cast great shadows, darkening the area under their foliage. There was no sign of a path.

Roland began trotting along again, conserving his strength. He had not gone twenty minutes more when suddenly his ears caught a faint sound. He stopped and listened with dread. It came again, and he muttered, "The dogs—they've picked up my trail!"

He plunged ahead through the thickness of the forest, hoping to find another stream where he might lose the dogs. There were no streams, however, and he thought their baying grew ever more powerful and strong.

A wild notion came to Roland then. He glanced up into the trees and thought of climbing one and going from tree to tree until he had lost the dogs. *They couldn't track me up there*, he thought. But he had no time to get far that way. And once he was up in a tree, he was trapped. He threw himself forward.

He came to a sharply crested wooded hill. His breath was coming in spasms now, but he struggled up the incline. Just as he got to the top he looked back to see the dogs, huge blue-colored animals, emerge from the thicker woods below. They sighted him and let loose a tremendous baying.

With no plan at all now, Roland ran along the crest, hoping to again find a place too thick for the horses—wherever they were—to follow the dogs. But the timber was thinning out, and he had to escape the dogs at once. He looked down the steep slope and started over the edge into the canyon below. He fell, rolling down the hill, his flesh scraped by sharp stones. When he got to the bottom, he scrambled to his feet and ran, but the hounds were already baying up on the ridge.

And then he came to a sheer stone wall and knew that he had run into a blind canyon. Whirling, he snatched up a dead branch to defend himself, the only weapon available. Now the dogs were in the canyon.

Backing into a niche in the canyon wall, Roland reversed the jagged end of the branch. When the first dog leaped at him, he rammed the branch as hard as he could into the animal's throat. The dog's baying was cut off, and he began rolling and choking.

But others were upon him. He fought them off by jabbing with the stick. Their howlings and barkings filled the air, and he knew then that the end was near.

"I'm trusting you, Goél," he gasped aloud, "even though I don't see any hope now."

And then Lord Zarak came into view. The lords accompanying him on the Hunt were strung out behind him.

The wizard reined in his horse, a cruel smile on his lips. "Well, we have found our quarry," he said as his followers galloped up.

"Will you kill him now, my lord?" Cranmore asked. He sounded worried. "Perhaps we had better wait. You know what the king's command was."

Zarak said, "We'll let the dogs kill him. That way we can say we intended to stop them."

The hunters sat on their horses watching as the dogs time and time again tried to get at Roland, but he fought them off valiantly.

"He's a fighter, my lord," the sheriff said. "He's got courage."

"Those mangy dogs!" Zarak cried. "Kill him! Kill him!"

Even as he shouted, someone behind Zarak cried, "It is the king and the Lady Lara, my lord!"

Zarak whirled in his saddle.

Roland, battling the dogs, was dimly aware that the king was indeed coming, leaning forward on his horse, urging him to full speed.

Then Lord Zarak grabbed his spear and put his spurs to his horse.

Completely exhausted, Roland saw the hounds scatter and heard Zarak's cry of rage.

The king's counselor, spear in hand, stopped not ten feet away. "You've had your run and now you die!" he screamed.

Roland saw the wizard's arm go back. He saw the spear plunge forward. It drove toward him so quickly that all he could do was twist his body. The spear tore through his clothing and raked across his chest. Roland grabbed up the spear. At least now he had a proper weapon. He knew that Zarak would be coming at him next with his sword.

Indeed, the wizard had drawn his sword, but even as he rushed toward Roland, an arrow pierced the fleshy part of Zarak's upper arm. Other arrows began hissing through the air. Zarak spun about to see his followers falling back.

Looking upward, Roland saw the edge of the canyon lined with bowmen in green. And then he heard someone shouting, "For Goél! For Goél!"

The king and the Lady Lara came off their horses, and she came running to him. "Roland," she cried, "are you all right?"

"I'm all right. What are you doing here?"

"You're bleeding," she whispered.

Roland looked down at his chest. "Nothing serious." Dazed, now he stared at the king, wondering what *he* was doing here.

But there King Falmor was, standing with drawn sword, watching Zarak, Cranmore, and the lords whirl to flee on their horses. Some appeared to be wounded. A few of their number were on the ground, lying still as dead men.

"Well, this battle is won," the king said. There was

a happy expression in his eyes. But then he said to Lady Lara, "You were right about Zarak. He is an evil man."

At that moment, Roland saw the last of the fleeing lords draw a bow and let fly an arrow toward them. It was surely accidental. He had no hope of hitting anything, but the arrow struck the king in the side. Falmor gave a cry and staggered back. He had received what could be a deadly wound.

"Father! You've been hurt!"

The king looked down at the arrow. "My daughter," he said weakly, "if I die, you will rule this kingdom. Do not let Zarak have any power over you."

"Father, you will get well! You can't die!"

"We've got to stop the bleeding," Roland cried.

A moment later Goodman and the Sleepers rushed up. Josh and Sarah were among them. Roland could not take it all in.

Josh knelt down beside the king. "This is a bad wound," he said. Goodman, who seemed to have had much experience with wounds, removed the arrow, but his face was grave. "Sometimes the lords put poison on their arrows, and the king looks deathly ill . . ."

"We must get him away from here," Josh said grimly, "If I know Zarak, he'll be back with the army."

"Yes. Make a litter, quick!" Goodman said.

Roland watched two of Goodman's followers trim saplings and use their outer garments to make a rough stretcher.

"Quick, now! We've got to get him away from this place!" Goodman urged. "We will go to Garn's home. Bentain is the best for treating wounds."

Four men carried the king. His face was pale, and his eyes were closed.

At Lady Lara's insistence, Roland, beginning to feel weak, mounted the king's stallion.

Then she mounted the mare, and side by side they rode behind the stretcher bearers. She looked at him, her face pale and her lips trembling. "He's got to be all right. He can't die."

But Roland knew how serious the wound was. "We'll hope for the best," he said. He suddenly reached over and took her hand. "You came for me," he whispered, and he lifted her hand and kissed it. Then he said, "Your father has proven himself to be noble indeed. Surely he will live to rule his people."

13
Evil Tidings

The trip through the forest seemed painfully long, and the Lady Lara could not keep her concern from showing. One time, when tears were running down her cheeks, Sarah rode beside her. The girl leaned over and put a hand on Lara's arm. "Take courage, my lady," she said quietly.

"But he might die!"

"We Sleepers have been through many dangerous times, and all of us have been wounded at one time or another. Always we have been kept safely by Goél. He does what is best even when we don't understand."

"But Goél is not here."

"He is not unaware, my lady, of your grief. You will see."

After a roundabout journey, the procession arrived at the house of Garn. They were met by Garn and his wife and old Bentain.

"The king is here," Goodman said quickly. "He must be cared for—he is grievously wounded."

"He must take over our house," Garn said. "It is poor enough, but he is welcome to all we have to offer."

Goodman nodded. "Make a bed ready for him, then. And, Bentain, you must see to his wound. I did the best I could."

Goodman supervised the moving of the king, and soon Bentain was tending to the wounded man. "It is a bad wound indeed," he said. But he glanced at Lady

Lara and said quickly, "Still, I have seen men with worse wounds recover."

"Let me do something to help," Lady Lara said.

"Sit beside him. That will help. I must go to the forest. There are certain herbs that, I think, will help his recovery."

The king moaned, and Lara immediately went to him. "Father," she said, "can you hear me?"

King Falmor's eyes opened. "Lara, is it you?"

"Yes. It is I. You've been wounded, Father. Try to lie still. You'll be well soon."

The king smiled faintly, but it was clear that pain was racing through him.

"I will return quickly," Bentain said, and he left the hut.

Lara attempted to comfort her father.

It was quiet in Garn's hut. She looked about and saw that the dwelling was a single room with rude furniture carved from wood. At one end was a rough fireplace where the cooking was done and which would give off heat in the cold weather. There was only this one bed in the house. A ladder led up to a loft. She had never been inside such a place before. She whispered in wonderment, "And a whole family lives here!"

A shadow fell across her then, and she looked around to see Sarah and Roland enter. They stood silently beside the bed, and Sarah asked, "How is he, my lady?"

"Bentain thinks the arrow must have been poisoned. He has gone to get something from the woods. Some sort of special healing herb." She looked up at them worriedly. "I couldn't bear it if anything happened to him."

She was sitting on a rough stool, and Roland knelt beside her. Now his eyes were even with hers. "Do not fear, Lady Lara," he said quietly. "You have friends here—and the Sleepers assure me that Goél has never failed. We must rely on him."

Unthinkingly Lady Lara reached out her free hand, and he took it in his. "Don't leave me, Roland," she said. "I'm so afraid."

"I won't leave," he promised.

Bentain returned after what seemed a long time. He said breathlessly, "I have found something that may help." He quickly heated water and made a brew in an iron pot. The smell of it filled the small house with a pleasant aroma. He kept the pot over the fire so that the steam rose steadily. "It will do him good just to breathe this, but he must also drink as much as possible."

It was difficult to get the king to drink, but Bentain insisted, "It is important that he drink a great deal of this." He managed to get a swallow down, but then the king jerked his arm and spilled the rest.

Bentain shook his head. "We must give it to him a sip at a time."

Even that proved to be difficult. Watching, Lara wondered at the kindness and concern shown by this old man of whom she had thought so little.

The hours went on, and Lara finally slumped on the stool. She felt herself being picked up, then realized that Roland was carrying her across the room. He placed her on a mattress. It was made of skins and seemed to be stuffed with straw.

"Sleep," he said. "We will care for your father."

"Don't leave me, Roland." She reached up her hand like a child, and he sat down beside her and held it.

* * *

When Sarah went outside Garn's small hut, she found all of the Sleepers gathered at the doorstep.

"How's the king?" Jake asked, and Sarah's eyes met his with discouragement. "He's worse, I think."

"Isn't there anything anybody can do?" Jake demanded. "If we only had a doctor!"

"I think most of the doctors around here wouldn't be much help for this . . . special kind of wound," Sarah said quietly.

Dave picked up on her words and her tone. "What are you thinking, Sarah?"

"That this is more than just an arrow wound. It's likely Zarak had his men use some sort of poison on the tip of the arrow, and I think that is what's killing the king. The wound itself wouldn't do it. It doesn't seem that serious."

"I do wish Goél were here," Abbey said, her eyes filled with grief. "He could help."

"That's what we're all hoping for," Josh said. "And if he doesn't come soon, the king may die."

"Well, one more time we'll just have to wait," Dave said.

"And I don't like waiting." Reb Jackson looked toward the forest with apprehension in his eyes. "If we get caught here by the soldiers of Lord Zarak, we'll all be goners. Not just the king."

That afternoon, Josh was by the door of Garn's house when Goodman came running. "I must see the Lady Lara!"

Lara came out at once with Roland by her side.

They had left Bentain and Garn's wife, they said, to minister to the king.

"I have evil tidings, my lady," Goodman reported. His face was twisted with both anger and worry.

"What is it?" Lady Lara asked.

"It's Lord Zarak, my lady."

"What's the wizard done now?" Roland demanded.

"He's announced to the people that the king is dead!"

"What!" Lady Lara cried. "How could he dare do that?"

"He knows what he's doing. If the king is dead, you are the next in line. And he has also announced that an evil group has kidnapped you after killing the king. The Seven Sleepers, he calls them. And, of course, my men and I are on his list of enemies, too. He says he's going to rescue you. Then he will marry you and rule over the kingdom."

"What do the people say?" Lady Lara asked, her eyes flashing. "Surely they can't believe that."

"I don't think most of them do. But it doesn't matter much whether they believe it or not," Goodman said sadly. "They hate Zarak, but he has the power."

"But what can we do?" Lady Lara exclaimed.

"How is the king?" Goodman said.

"Not well," Roland answered.

"I trust that he will be well soon," Goodman said, "but if he does not survive, what will you do, Lady Lara?"

The princess drew herself up defiantly and said, "I will never marry that evil man! Never!"

"Then you are in great danger. I fear that if you refuse to marry Lord Zarak, you too will meet with an 'accident,'" he said, stressing the word "accident." He added grimly, "Then the blame for that too could be put upon the Seven Sleepers and me."

"That's exactly what he'll do, Lady Lara!" Roland exclaimed.

Josh was trying to think what the next step should be. "What else did you learn, Goodman?" he asked.

"That Lord Zarak is summoning all of his men. They'll be sweeping the forest soon and looking behind every tree." His voice was still grim. "Sooner or later they'll find us, and we're too few in number to fight such an army."

Lady Lara then proved herself to be, indeed, a princess. She stood straight, and her eyes went to Goodman. "You have been a faithful servant, Goodman." She looked around at her friends, and there was warmth in her look. "All of you Sleepers, I thank you for your kindness. You came to do us good, and you have received an ill reception."

"We want to serve you, lady," Josh said. "What shall we do?"

"Is there any place where we can move my father that would be safer than here?"

Goodman rubbed his chin, thinking, but then shook his head. "This is as safe a place as any. My men and I will try to discover the movements of Zarak. If the enemy comes this way, then we will have to flee."

Lara nodded. "So we can only pray that my father will regain his strength. I must go to him now."

The Sleepers watched her go back into the house.

"She's changed a lot, hasn't she?" Roland said quietly.

"She has. And so have you, Roland." Josh grinned at him.

"Me!" Roland looked surprised. "Oh . . . well . . . I suppose I have. Being a slave teaches you things!"

Lady Lara learned much over the next two days. While she nursed her father, she got to know the family of Garn and his wife. She learned to love their two children. But the biggest change of all was that great pity came into her heart as she saw the poverty and fear in which they were forced to live.

"If my father and I ever rule again," she told Roland late one evening, "things will be different. People like Garn and his family will be the object of our care. You will see!" She turned to him and asked earnestly, "Do you believe that, Roland?"

He nodded. "I believe it now. As Josh said, you have changed. And I have changed." Then he seemed to remember something. "It's the hard things, my father always said, that make people strong. If this hadn't happened to me, I suppose I would have gone on being the same selfish person that I've always been."

"Your father sounds like a wise man," Lady Lara said. "I hope to meet him one day."

Roland took her hand. "I hope, indeed, that you will."

The princess said no more, and together they sat looking down at the pale face of the king who struggled for life.

14

A Small Miracle

Each day Lady Lara and the Sleepers lived in constant apprehension over the movements of Lord Zarak. Messengers came secretly from Goodman, who had his men tracking Zarak's army—and usually they brought bad news.

"It is terrible," one messenger said, a tall fellow named Coaltar. "Zarak is even far more cruel than we had believed."

"What is he doing?" Lady Lara asked.

"He is taking many hostages. He is throwing old people and young alike into the foul dungeons of the castle. He keeps spreading the rumors that the king has been slain by the Seven Sleepers and that you are held captive by them."

Josh, who had been standing by, exclaimed, "We've got to do something about Zarak!"

Coaltar turned to him. "Why does he hate you Sleepers so much?"

"How do you know that he does?" Josh asked curiously.

"We have one sympathizer in his ranks. He tells us that Zarak seems to go mad whenever the Seven Sleepers are mentioned. Don't let him take you alive," Coaltar warned. "You will die slowly and in agony. But why does he hate you so?"

"Because we are the servants of Goél and he is an instrument of the Dark Lord."

"Such things are too high for me," Coaltar said, "but you would do well to stay out of his clutches."

Lady Lara waited only until Coaltar left, and then she went back to sit beside her father. She took a quick breath for he lay very still, but when she laid her hand on his chest, she felt the slight rise and fall of his breathing. For a long time she sat beside him.

Roland came in after a while and sat across from her. "How is he?"

"He is worse. I fear he is dying, Roland."

Roland did not disagree. Instead, he studied Lara's face and seemed to be trying to find words that might encourage her. Perhaps he decided to turn her thoughts to something else, for at last he said, "I can't stop thinking about what I was before I came on this mission."

"What do you mean, Roland?"

Roland shifted his weight on the stool. "I mean that I was the most selfish human being that ever lived."

Lara was able to smile briefly. "I doubt that," she said. "I believe I was."

He managed a smile, too. "But you don't know what I was like. I thought only of myself; I was a bully. Anyone smaller, anyone that I could push around, I did. I don't see how my parents or anyone else stood me."

"You might be describing me," Lady Lara said. Then she added, "I intend my life to be different from now on, though."

"I'm glad to hear that."

Both Lara and Roland jumped to their feet. Somehow the princess knew who the speaker was as soon as she saw him.

Goél's hood was shading his face, and he pushed it back.

Without a word, the two knelt before him.

Goél put one hand on Lara's head, the other on Roland's, and kept them there a moment. Then he said, "Rise up, my children. You indeed are passing through a deep valley."

"Goél, my father is dying!" Lara looked up at him pleadingly.

He took her hands and said, "Do not fear, Lady Lara."

Somehow she could sense the man's strength. She had heard much about Goél from Roland and Bentain and Sarah. Now she found she could barely speak to him. She finally whispered, "I have been wicked, sire, but I want to be different."

"You are already different, and you will grow as time passes."

"But my father, Goél. He is dying."

Goél dropped her hands then and sat on the stool beside the king's bed. For a time he simply sat looking into the pale face of King Falmor, as Lara and Roland watched him.

Goél put one hand on King Falmor's forehead. At his touch the king suddenly stiffened, and he moaned.

Goél leaned toward the king and spoke words that Lara could not hear. His voice had been quiet, almost a whisper.

Sudden shock ran through Lara then. As she watched, color began coming back into her father's face. And then with joy she saw his eyelids flutter and his lips move slightly.

"You have been under a dark cloud for many years, my friend."

This time she did hear Goél's quiet voice. It was filled with power and warmth, and it seemed to affect the king's entire body.

King Falmor's eyes flew open, and his gaze met that of Goél.

"Who are you, sire?"

"I am Goél."

The king lay still, but then his eyes fell on Lara. He held out his hand, and she flew at once to take it. "Father, you're better!"

The king muttered, "I am better. How long have I been here?"

"You have been in this bed only a few days," Goél told him. He stood now and looked down on the king. "But you have been under the power of an evil force for many years. Your spirit is weary. As for the wound, you will find that it will properly heal now. I have dealt with the poison."

"I have strength again!" the king exclaimed. "I want to sit up." With Roland's help he managed to sit in the bed, and then he stared long at the boy. "I remember. Your name is Roland."

"Yes, sire."

"He has been a faithful servant to you, King Falmor," Goél said. His eyes went to Lara, and he added, "I think you will find a way to reward him."

The king stood to his feet shakily. He faced Goél and bowed his head. "I fear I have not been a good king, sire."

"You have been controlled by an evil force, but it is not too late to change."

King Falmor then looked at Lara. "Indeed, your mother would have hated what I have become."

"It will be different now, Father."

"Yes, it will."

Josh and the other Sleepers and Goodman were waiting by the door of the hut when Goél came out.

"How is the king?" Josh asked at once.

"The king will get well."

A cheer went up, and Josh said, "It's a miracle!"

Goél smiled. "A small miracle perhaps." Then his face grew serious. "But there is still a battle to fight."

"You told us the battle would mostly be in the hearts of people," Sarah said quietly. "And now the king's heart is changed, and Lady Lara's heart is changed, and—"

"Yes. But evil must be rooted out of the land. Lord Zarak will kill you all if he has the chance."

Goodman said, "All of my men are ready, sire, but what are we against so many?"

"Strength is not always in numbers. There once lived a wise man who delivered a whole city into the hands of an army. I think we will see another 'small miracle,' but you must fight," Goél said. "The heart of the king has indeed changed, and when he is on his throne again and evil is defeated, this land will see peace and justice."

Sarah was standing next to Josh, and he felt her take his hand. Then he heard her whisper, "And I'll bet we see a new prince very soon, too."

"What are you talking about?"

"Oh, you're so dense, Joshua Adams! I mean Lady Lara will marry Roland."

"How do you know *that?*"

Sarah was feeling very good. "I didn't read all those romances for nothing. They'll get married and live happily ever after."

He laughed. "You are a romantic, Sarah."

"Yes, I am," she said firmly. "And it wouldn't hurt you to have a little more romance in your soul."

15
Lord Zarak's Castle

I'm worried," Reb said. "I'm really worried." He was sharpening his sword, and he looked apprehensively toward the dark forest that surrounded the farm of Garn.

"What are you worried about now?" Wash asked. He was eating a raw turnip, and he frowned at it. "I guess some people like raw turnips—but I don't think I could stand many more of them."

"You're always thinking about your stomach," Reb said. "Why don't you think about the big problem?"

"What big problem?"

Reb cast a look of disgust toward his smaller friend. "I mean that the forest out there is crawling with Zarak's army. They could come busting in here at any minute. I sure wish we had a bunch of Stonewall Jackson's soldiers here."

"Well, we don't. We've got a few men in green under Goodman, and we've got us. How many do you suppose Lord Zarak has?"

"More than a thousand, I suppose." But Reb suddenly grinned. "Well, that sounds about right—us against a thousand. We can take 'em, don't you think?"

Wash finally threw the turnip away, saying, "I wish I had a boloney sandwich and an RC Cola."

"Don't talk like that," Reb groaned. "What wouldn't I give for a Quarter Pounder and a chocolate milkshake! But those days are gone. Tell you what, though. If we don't get into action pretty soon, I'm gonna go out and kill us a wild pig or something. Might as well kill one of the king's deer while I'm at it. What could Zarak do to us that he's not planning to do already—which is to hang us?"

Josh and Sarah came wandering up. Josh asked, "What are you two doing?"

"Eating raw turnips and hating them," Wash said. "My stomach thinks my throat's been cut."

"I was talking about going out and getting us a deer," Reb said.

Josh grinned. "Might as well. Zarak would kill us anyway."

Reb leaped up. "Well, I'm glad you agree. You want to come, too, Wash?"

"No. I'll just stay here and dream about eating."

"Some good venison stew would be good for the king," Sarah said. "Or even venison steak!"

"How is he?" Wash inquired.

"He's getting stronger every day. It really was a miracle how that wound started to get better."

"It was the poison that was the big problem," Lady Lara said. "And Goél did something about that. Which reminds me. If we go into battle again, we'd better be careful. Nothing to slow a fellow down like poisoned arrows."

At that point Dave and Abbey joined them. "What comes next?" Dave said. "We can't hide here forever."

"We're bound to get discovered sooner or later, aren't we?" Abbey asked nervously.

"And what's happened to Goél?" Dave went on. "I haven't seen him for two days now."

"He disappeared after he helped the king, but they had a long talk together, I understand," Josh said.

"What did they talk about?" Wash asked eagerly.

"They didn't let me in on their plans, but I feel better about everything now—even if there are a thousand guys out there wanting to kill us."

They were still talking when Reb came back with a deer slung over the back of the workhorse. "Supper time!" he said. "Let's skin this critter and eat!"

Roland, as well as Goodman, joined the Seven Sleepers, Lady Lara, and King Falmor for a meal of delicious venison steaks cooked over an open fire.

Roland thought the king was looking much better today.

Falmor ate his steak eagerly. "This is the best feast I've had in memory," he said.

Lady Lara laughed. "Hunger is a good sauce, isn't it? Who killed this deer?"

"Well, I reckon I did," Reb said.

"I thank you for your generosity, Reb."

The king smiled. "Perhaps we ought to dub you Sir Reb."

"Oh, he's already Sir Reb. He was made that by the king of Camelot," Wash said warmly, his eyes full of admiration for his friend. "How do you feel, Your Majesty?"

"I feel like a new man. Not just physically but inside too." Then the king saw Garn and his family returning from a day in the woods, looking for berries. He called, "Come and join us."

"Oh, no, Your Majesty!" Garn said.

"And I say yes! Come. And you, boy, what's your name?"

"Robert."

"Come, Robert. And you?"

"My name is Pilar."

"Come. We're all one here."

Garn and his wife and children came forward shyly.

After watching all of this, Roland leaned over and whispered to Lady Lara, "I'm sure they never expected to ever eat with the king!"

"Just look at their eyes, Roland. You can see they love him."

"I think now that he's himself again, all of his people will love him."

When all had finished eating, Josh said, "Your Majesty, it's very dangerous here."

"I realize that, my friend Josh, and I have devised a plan."

"A plan, Your Majesty?" Roland said. "You mean a plan to defeat Lord Zarak or—"

"Yes. He must be defeated. He's already announced that I am dead, and if he catches me, I will be dead indeed. When my daughter refuses to marry him, she will perish, also."

Josh nodded. "I'm sure you're right. But we're just so mightily outnumbered . . ."

"We are badly outnumbered, indeed, but knowledge is power," King Falmor said. "And I know one thing that gives us an advantage."

"What is that, Father?" Lady Lara asked curiously. She was so proud of her father. He had changed completely, and now he looked every inch a king.

"There is a way. We must get at Zarak, and we cannot do it in open battle on the field. That means we must get to him in the castle."

"But it would take an army to storm that castle!" Josh protested. "It would have to be besieged for months!"

"That is true," Goodman said, "although we will try if you insist, Your Majesty. But it would seem hopeless."

"You're right. A siege would be hopeless. But suppose there were a secret way into the castle?"

"Is there?" Roland exclaimed.

"Indeed there is such a way." The king's eyes sparkled as he explained. "My great-grandfather built this castle. He foresaw the time when there might be a need for someone inside to escape if the castle was besieged. So he made a secret passage. It was never used, but he passed the secret down to my grandfather, who gave it to my father, and my father gave it to me."

"All right!" Reb Jackson cried. "Lead me to it!"

Roland was thinking hard. "Most of the army is out trying to find us. Isn't that right, Goodman?"

"That is right. Lord Zarak stays in the castle with just a small guard. He doesn't think he needs much protection from a ragtag bunch such as we are."

"He will find out what we are," King Falmor said, "when we take both the castle and him." He stood up. "Let us prepare to go immediately. Can you lead us through the forest, avoiding Zarak's army, Goodman?"

"I can do it, sire."

"Then get your men together. We will start at once."

Excitement ran through the small camp. The Sleepers gathered up their weapons. Their guide, Goodman, sent out scouts to make sure they were not interrupted. And soon the king and his daughter headed a procession.

As they tramped along, Lady Lara's eyes went often to Roland.

One time Sarah saw her watching the tall boy. "He is handsome, isn't he, my lady?"

"Yes. You said that once before. And I have come to see something very good *within* him as well."

The king called a halt when they reached the river. "Now," he said, "we must be very careful and wait until dark."

"That will be in less than an hour, Your Majesty," Goodman said, glancing at the sky.

"We must not be discovered here. And when we do move, we must move very quietly." Then Lara's father laughed aloud. "But I am saying that to myself. Your men move as silently as deer. I am the one who is clumsy."

Darkness fell, and when the moon rose high enough to give them light, King Falmor said, "Let us go. The entrance is this way." He walked ahead, and soon the entire party found themselves at the foot of a cliff. High overhead the castle reared into the sky.

"We can never climb up there," Dave muttered.

"We will not have to climb," the king said. "Follow me." He led them then to where the foot of the mountain was covered with thick brush. "I haven't been to this place since I was a boy, but it's here. It's here." Soon he cried, "And see! Here it is."

Lady Lara was right behind her father. "Why, there's an opening—like a cave opening."

"The tunnel was cut out of solid rock. As you see, the entrance is narrow, admitting only one at a time. But then the passage widens."

"Let me go first, sire," Roland said. "If there's danger, you must be protected."

The king looked about to protest, then said, "Very well. You first, and I will follow. Then you, my daughter."

They cut pine boughs, rich in pitch, and lit them as

144

torches. Then, one by one, they slipped through the entrance and began winding their way upward through a twisting passage. It was often a low and narrow tunnel, and at places even Lara had to duck.

And then Roland, who was still in the lead, said softly over his shoulder, "Your Majesty, we've come to a door."

"It is the secret door to my quarters," the king said. "On the other side it does not look to be a door."

King Falmor waited until the Sleepers and Goodman crowded closer. "Pass along the word to put out the torches. We don't know who is on the other side of this door," he said in a low voice. "Probably no one, since it is my private chamber. We will go inside and then gather ourselves and go directly to the quarters of Zarak. When we have captured him, the rest will be simple."

Josh found himself breathing hard, and he whispered to Sarah, "Once again we're headed into danger. Be careful, Sarah. I don't want anything to happen to you."

Sarah reached out and squeezed his hand. "You be careful, too, Josh."

The king stepped around Roland and opened the secret door. It slid back silently, revealing a lighted room. Josh was ready to follow Roland and Lady Lara through the doorway when the king spoke in a loud voice.

"Zarak! So you've taken over the king's quarters, have you?"

Lord Zarak leaped to his feet. His eyes flew wide with shock, and he cried out for his guards as he drew his sword.

The king drew his own sword, and the two began to duel as the Sleepers and then Goodman's men poured into the large chamber.

"The guards are coming!" Lara cried.

And then, within the confines of the king's quarters, a bitter fight took place. King Falmor was an older man than Lord Zarak and recently wounded. Still, he seemed to gain strength as he fought. While the others dealt with the guards, the king backed Zarak against the wall and tore the sword from his hand with one mighty stroke.

He put his sword point right under Zarak's heart, and for a moment Josh thought he would kill him. He held his breath, but then the king lowered his blade.

"You are an evil man, Zarak, but I will not kill you. There's been enough killing already. You are my prisoner."

Lord Zarak's few guards had been totally unprepared. The Sleepers and Goodman and his men in green swarmed through the castle, taking it by storm. Less than an hour later Josh was standing in the castle's large banquet hall, where the king had gathered his followers.

Falmor looked about at them all, his eyes warm. "You have all served your king well, and you will find me to be grateful." His eyes went to Lara then, and he smiled. "My first act will be to open the dungeons and free every prisoner!"

A cheer went up from Goodman. A cheer went up from his men. Josh saw Lady Lara take Roland's hand.

The king too saw this. He walked over to them, and for a moment he frowned. But then he said, "I see that I am to have a son at last after all these years?"

"I would serve Your Majesty always, but I must tell you that I love your daughter."

"And I love him, Father."

"We shall have time to get to know each other, Sir Roland."

"I am no 'sir,' Your Majesty," Roland said quickly.

"You are now. My daughter could not marry a commoner, so I dub you Sir Roland."

Another cheer went up, and the Sleepers did a dance about the floor. Josh found himself holding Sarah's hand, and they whirled in a wild circle. Dave, not to be outdone, grabbed Abbey's hand and they too spun around.

When the merriment had ceased, the king said, "We will deal with Zarak, but he will not receive from my hand all of what he deserves."

"I think Goél would approve of that, sire," Josh said. "There's hope even for a man like Lord Zarak."

The king looked at Josh and then at the other Sleepers. "Will you all stay on as our guests?"

"As long as possible," Josh said. "We always are at the will of Goél."

"Very good. Then we will have a feast, and we will proclaim liberty to the captives." His voice rose as he said, "And now the people of my kingdom will know a ruler who has generosity." He put his arm around his daughter and drew her close. "And the Lady Lara will show goodness and love to all of her people."

"Well," Josh said to Sarah, "it looks like the storybooks were right. They're going to live happily ever after."

16

An Adventure Ends

The kingdom of Falmor knew peace and joy that had been only a memory to some of the older men and women. The king moved among his people, smiling and greeting them, and daily he listened to their needs as they came before him. Always at his right hand was his daughter, the Lady Lara. And always close beside her was Sir Roland Winters, who would be the prince and the future king.

The Sleepers enjoyed themselves tremendously as the days passed. They hunted. They fished. They rode with the hounds. None enjoyed all this more than Reb Jackson. He proved himself to be the best horseman in the land. When he braided a rope and performed before the court—bringing down a wild bull by throwing a loop around its front legs—the entire kingdom idolized Sir Reb.

"Have you noticed that little redheaded lady who watches you so closely?" Roland asked Reb one day.

"Oh, I don't pay any attention to things like that," Reb muttered.

"Her father is a powerful lord. If you wanted to, I think you could marry her and become a very important man in the kingdom of Falmor."

"I'm a very important man already," Reb said. "I'm one of the Seven Sleepers."

Roland grinned. "I didn't think you'd be interested. How long will you all be staying, do you think?"

"Don't know. And I suppose you're not going back with us."

"Uh . . . no," Roland said absently.

Later that day he was walking along the parapet of the castle with Lady Lara. They stopped and looked out over the green fields, which were beautiful indeed. In the distance smoke was rising from farm house chimneys, and white clouds drifted lazily overhead. "You know," he said, "I must go back and make things right with my parents."

"I knew you would say that someday." The princess hesitated, biting her lower lip. "I will miss you."

"I would ask you to accompany me, but it wouldn't be proper for a princess to travel alone with a man for such a long way."

Lady Lara lifted her eyebrows. "And can you think of no way to make it proper?"

For a moment Roland was surprised. He laughed. "I can think of one way. If we were married, then traveling together would be perfectly proper."

Lara waited, then said impatiently, "Well?"

"Well what?"

"Well, are you not going to propose?"

"I *am* going to propose. I want to marry you. I'll be the best husband to you I can be—if you'll have me."

Far down the castle parapet, Josh and Sarah stood watching Roland and the princess. "We really shouldn't be snooping like this!" he protested.

"Don't be silly!" Sarah said dreamily. "If they don't want to be seen, they should have hidden themselves."

Josh shrugged. "Well, they evidently don't care who sees them. I guess that settles that."

"It's just like a fairy tale, isn't it, Josh?"

"I don't know. I haven't lived many of those."

"Then your education's been neglected."

They watched until Lady Lara and Roland walked on, and then Josh said, "Well, Sarah, we're about to the end of another adventure."

"There's another one coming, though. Goél always sees to that. He keeps life interesting."

It was later in the afternoon when Goél suddenly appeared to the Seven Sleepers and told them, "The eagles await, my young friends."

The Sleepers, as always, were happy to see him. They said, "We'll have to say our good-byes to the king and the court."

"Any farewells must be brief. There's an emergency. You must come quickly."

"Well, I like that!" Jake muttered as they set off to find their friends. "Out of the frying pan and into the fire. Probably have to go kill a few dragons, Reb."

Josh and Sarah said quick good-byes to the princess and to Roland, who grinned and said, "You'll come back someday, won't you?"

"We would be happy to. But you never know when you follow Goél," Josh said. "We let him give the directions. Good-bye, Lady Lara. Good-bye, Roland."

Goél led the Seven Sleepers to where Kybus and the great birds were waiting. "Go quickly now, and I will meet you and give you more instructions."

Josh went over to where Sarah was about to mount her eagle. "Let me help you," he said. He put his hand down as he had seen squires do. But when she put her foot in it, he heaved so strongly that she flew over the eagle and landed on her back with a grunt.

"Sarah, I didn't mean to do that!" He rushed around

to help her up and began to dust her off. He was sure she would be angry.

But instead she laughed. "That's all right, Josh. I'm not hurt. Let's try it again—but a little more gently this time."

He put both hands down and carefully lifted her into the saddle. Then he took her hand and kissed it. "There," he said. "Is that romantic enough?"

Sarah blushed. "It'll do for starters," she said.

And soon the air was filled with the sound of beating wings as the eagles rose toward the sky, carrying the Seven Sleepers into their next adventure.

Get swept away in the many Gilbert Morris Adventures available from Moody Press:

Seven Sleepers Series

3681-1 Flight of the Eagles
3682-X The Gates of Neptune
3683-3 The Swords of Camelot
3684-6 The Caves That Time Forgot
3685-4 Winged Riders of the Desert
3686-2 Empress of the Underworld
3687-0 Voyage of the Dolphin
3691-9 Attack of the Amazons
3692-7 Escape with the Dream Maker
3693-5 The Final Kingdom

Go with Josh and his friends as they are sent by Goél, their spiritual leader, on dangerous and challenging voyages to conquer the forces of darkness in the new world. Ages 10-14

Bonnets and Bugles Series

0911-3 Drummer Boy at Bull Run
0912-1 Yankee Bells in Dixie
0913-X The Secret of Richmond Manor
0914-8 The Soldier Boy's Discovery
0915-6 Blockade Runner
0916-4 The Gallant Boys of Gettysburg
0917-2 The Battle of Lookout Mountain
0918-0 Encounter at Cold Harbor
0919-9 Fire Over Atlanta
0920-2 Bring the Boys Home

Follow good friends Leah Carter and Jeff Majors as they experience danger, intrigue, compassion, and love in these civil war adventures. Ages 10-14

Dixie Morris Animal Adventures

3363-4 Dixie and Jumbo
3364-2 Dixie and Stripes
3365-0 Dixie and Dolly
3366-9 Dixie and Sandy
3367-7 Dixie and Ivan
3368-5 Dixie and Bandit
3369-3 Dixie and Champ
3370-7 Dixie and Perry
3371-5 Dixie and Blizzard
3382-3 Dixie and Flash

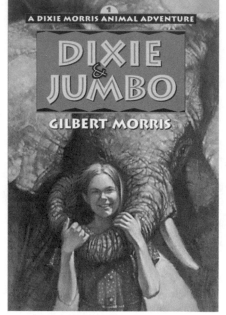

Follow the exciting adventures of this animal lover as she learns more of God and His character through her many adventures underneath the Big Top. Ages 9-14

The Daystar Voyages

4102-X Secret of the Planet Makon
4106-8 Wizards of the Galaxy
4107-6 Escape From the Red Comet
4108-4 Dark Spell Over Morlandria
4109-2 Revenge of the Space Pirates
4110-6 Invasion of the Killer Locusts
4111-4 Dangers of the Rainbow Nebula
4112-2 The Frozen Space Pilot

Join the crew of the Daystar as they traverse the wide expanse of space. Adventure and danger abound, but they learn time and again that God is truly the Master of the Universe. Ages 10-14

"Too Smart" Jones
4025-8 Pool Part Thief
4026-6 Buried Jewels
4027-4 Disappearing Dogs
4028-2 Dangerous Woman
4029-0 Stranger in the Cave
4030-4 Cat's Secret

Come along for the adventures and mysteries Juliet "Too Smart" Jones always manages to find. She and her other homeschool friends solve these great adventures and learn biblical truths along the way. Ages 9-14

Seven Sleepers - The Lost Chronicles
3667-6 The Spell of the Crystal Chair
3668-4 The Savage Game of Lord Zarak
3669-2 The Strange Creatures of Dr. Korbo
3670-6 City of the Cyborgs

More exciting adventures from the Seven Sleepers. As these exciting young people attempt to faithfully follow Goel, they learn important moral and spiritual lessons. Come along with them as they encounter danger, intrigue, and mystery. Ages 10-14